Suddenly a bright flash of flame burst from the engine. Martha's hands darted over the instrument panel as she flipped switches. White foam from the fire extinguisher spattered on the windshield as the engine died. She spun around to look at me. "Is your pack attached to the leg straps?" I stared at her. I couldn't move. I couldn't speak.

She heaved herself halfway over the seat back and with expert hands snapped the pack in place. "Keep your hand on the D-ring right here. Don't pull until you're out the door, then pull hard." In a quieter voice, she asked, "Do you understand?"

My mouth worked but no sound came out.

She leaned over to the far door and jerked at the latches. The door fell away. The rush of cold air made me gasp.

Martha turned back to me again. "Unsnap your seat belt." I did as she said. "Good luck, Lisa." Her hands half-lifted and half-shoved me toward the open door. "Now!" There was a lurch of the plane, a blast of cold air, and I felt myself falling.

Blind panic engulfed me.

WALKING OUT

by
Ann Elwood
& John Raht

tempo books
GROSSET & DUNLAP
A Filmways Company
Publishers • New York

Walking Out
Copyright © 1979 by Ann Elwood & John Raht
All Rights Reserved
ISBN: 0-448-17080-9
A Tempo Books Original
Tempo Books is registered in the U.S. Patent Office
Published simultaneously in Canada
Printed in the United States of America

WALKING OUT

Chapter One

I gazed out the plane window at the thick clouds below and let my thoughts drift to the last months of the school year that had ended in June. All of us —my friend B.J., Kyle, Dave, and I—had made our summer plans then. The big August beach party, B.J.'s sixteenth birthday party, the weekend sailing trip to Catalina. I'd miss out on every one of those big events. Instead, I'd be on a backpacking trip with my father in Alaska. I hadn't been too wild about the idea of camping out when Dad first brought it up, but it did have its advantages. If nothing else, I might lose weight, perhaps even that last ten pounds that stood between me and what I thought was perfection. I looked down at my legs, stretched to the footrest. My thighs in the new Calvin Klein jeans were fat—definitely fat!

"Your thighs are *not* fat," my mother had said when I complained about them. "Just chunky. You have a chunky build like me."

"Chunky!" I said in disgust. I had looked over at B.J., my best friend, who was sprawling in a chair.

Her casual posture and even more casual clothes could not hide the elegance of her long, thin body. "If you really loved me, Mother, you'd get me a build like B.J.'s."

B.J. had answered with a rare joke: "If you're chunky, then I'm stringy. Let's say you're voluptuous."

"That doesn't help, B.J.," I said.

Mother, who sensed I was having trouble with Kyle, tried to shore up my confidence and to make me laugh at myself. "Look at the plusses," she had said, walking over to sit facing me in the big leather chair by the fireplace. "Beautiful hair, a good mind, at least on occasion . . ."

"And not one zit!" B.J. had interrupted. "Do you know what most of us would do for that?"

My mother had quickly added: "If Lisa keeps eating junk foods, she'll be able to join the Zit Gang, too, and make herself even chunkier in the process."

I had clapped my hand to my head in an overdramatic gesture that I knew my mother would appreciate and the more prosaic B.J. would merely tolerate. "It is only the abuse of my family and friends that drives me to overdose with Twinkies and glazed doughnuts. In fact, I'd kill for a Twinkie at this very moment." I had settled for an apple.

The stewardess interrupted my thoughts of food with lunch. "Here you are," she said, sliding the plastic tray onto the little fold-down table in front of me.

I looked the lunch over, trying to figure out what B.J.—a health-food nut—would think of it. I decided she would have approved of everything on the airline's menu except the white bread in the cheese sandwich and the tempting chocolate brownie, which, crowned with thick, combed-looking, white icing, was sitting on the corner of the tray. I started to eat.

B.J.—I owed a lot to her. She had been the one to give me that extra push that made me go out for the track team my sophomore year. It was my first try at sports. I had expected to hate it, but all the other kids I hung around with were trying out for something, and I didn't want to be left out. To my surprise, it was fun. The conditioning exercises had made my body strong and supple. In the end, I was chosen for the relay and the javelin throw. The javelin was my favorite. I enjoyed the measured way in which the approach was taken, the poised balance, the dancelike steps just before the explosive final thrust. It all felt natural to me—more natural than the modern dance or boring exercise classes I had tried.

Kyle hadn't been impressed with my sports scene, and I had hoped he would be. He had been more impressed with Kathy, had he hadn't shown up at any of the meets. An image came into my mind—I tried to push it away, but it stayed: Kyle, the last week before finals, walking arm in arm with Kathy, his dark, curly hair covering his handsome face as he leaned to tell her something in that soft voice I knew all too well . . . . Oh, well, Dave had come to every meet. The thought of Dave on the sidelines had made me feel better.

Dave was someone new in my life. During that school year, he had moved to town from Dennison, Colorado. I had met him in my geometry class. He was tall and quiet, and seemed shy. His hair, which was short, made him stand out as a newcomer. But I liked him. I had been going steady with Kyle then. Once when I was walking along the beach with B.J., I had said that Dave was nice, but I was glad I was going steady with Kyle, and she had answered, "Isn't it too bad Kyle isn't going steady with you?" I had been furious with her. I was in love with Kyle, or maybe it was just that he had brought out feelings in me I hadn't really known were there, though I had gone steady with boys before. "How far did you go with him?" B.J. had asked. "Not *far* far," I had answered, "but pretty far." "Be careful," she had answered.

Kyle would sometimes tease me about Dave. One time when I was giving Kyle a hard time about the way he came on to other girls, he had said, "If you don't like it, why don't you go out with that hick, Dave?"

Angry, I had lashed back, "I bet you don't have the nerve to call him a hick to his face!"

The pilot's crisp voice broke into the scene in my head as he warned us over the loudspeakers to keep our seat belts fastened while we were in our seats. He added that we would be in Juneau in about thirty minutes. People started walking up and down the aisles of the plane to go to the bathrooms. I looked out the window. The cloud cover had broken, and we had dropped in altitude. I could see the deep green of the forests below, much greener than anything I ever saw in the hills around L.A., except where it was irrigated. No wonder my father loved it!

The stewardess stopped again at my seat to pick up the lunch tray. I looked at the brownie and at first decided to leave it, but then I changed my mind. I wrapped the brownie in the paper napkin from the tray and put it in my pocket. I left the half sandwich I hadn't eaten lying there.

As the stewardess picked up the tray, the big plane hit several good bumps in a row. "You might mention to the pilot that the sky's in need of repair," I said.

"It's like that this time of year," she answered, bending down to glance out the window. "But I'll tell him. He can take it up with the powers that be."

"I thought that flying this high, we'd be out of most of it."

"That's usually true," she said. "It's just that the weather around here can change so quickly that sometimes the pilot has to guess about the best altitude and speed."

She turned to answer a question from a passenger across the aisle, and I remembered my father's comment about Alaska, "Everything's bigger than life up there," he had said, "even the weather." That had been during his last visit to L.A. to see me, and it had made me happy to see his eyes light up when he talked about the wilderness, where his work as a diesel engine service salesman had taken him. I was glad because not much else seemed to be going well for him. The crow's feet around his eyes were deeper, and he looked more tired.

My father. He was familiar and unfamiliar to me. Familiar, since I had known him all my life, unfamiliar because he was away so much, traveling because of his job. Each time I saw him now, a few months had gone by, and sometimes he seemed like a different person. I was sure that a lot of this was because *I* was the one who was changing. There were times I thought he'd shrunk, then I'd realize that it was only that I had grown taller. When he and Mother were first divorced, I had seen him more often, but as time went on, the pressures of his job had increased, and he had to travel more, so we'd spent less time together.

I'd mentioned to Mother that he looked tired, and she didn't say anything, but I noticed that when we all went out to dinner together, she was especially kind to him. Sitting at the restaurant table, I noticed that he looked older—he'll be forty! I thought. It brought back memories of when I was little and we flew kites together on the beach. Then he could outrun me; maybe now I could outrun him. I wasn't sure I wanted to find out.

And when he had started talking about Alaska and our going backpacking together, he was so enthusiastic that I couldn't say no. "Remember when you came up to stay with me in San Francisco?" he had said. "And we met skiing at Tahoe? I remember how you love the outdoors, Lisa."

I hadn't wanted to tell him that it wasn't the outdoors I had liked so much about the ski trip, but the lodge with its big log fires, the glamorous people, and the fantastic food.

When I had told Dave about the backpacking trip, he had expressed the excitement I should have felt, but didn't. "That's great!" he had said. "Listen, I've got a lot of gear you can borrow. We used to backpack all the time in Colorado." When I'd told him thanks, but that my dad had sent me money for equipment, he had volunteered to help me pick it out. He and my mother and I had gone to the big sporting goods store in L.A. that specialized in backpacking. It was the first time that Mother had met Dave, and I was curious to see what she would say. I could tell she was impressed with his assurance when he talked about the equipment, by his knowledge of backpacking, and by his enthusiasm in helping me pick things out. She didn't say much until she and I went into one of the fitting rooms so I could try on some of the pants. We were talking about the clothes when she abruptly changed the subject. "Is it just possible that having Dave here means you have dumped that hood?"

"What hood?" "Kyle?" I kept looking at myself in the fitting-room mirror.

"Who else?"

"Mother, there aren't any hoods anymore. They're only in the movies or in reruns on TV. No guy these days greases back his hair and wears a motorcycle jacket. That was your era."

She didn't give up. "He's a hood at heart."

When I didn't answer, she switched to Dave. "I hate to say this, because I'm afraid it might be the kiss of death, but Dave seems like a nice guy."

I had to smile to myself, because even a year before, if Mother had said someone was a nice guy, it would have turned me off. Now I just said, "Yeah, he is," and let it go at that.

The air got rougher as we circled before landing. I looked down and I could see the bay curving in, with the tall trees of the forest running down almost to the water's edge. As we dropped a little more, the sun's rays hit the water and turned it silver.

The landing was a little bumpy, then the taxiing plane slowed as we approached the terminal building that looked so small compared to L.A.'s huge airport with its rows of buildings. I reviewed in my mind my list of belongings. My down jacket was stowed in the overhead, with my baggage check in the pocket. Everything else was in the heavy blue pack I had checked through. The book and the plane ticket for the connecting flight! I had put them in the elastic-topped pocket on the back seat in front of me. The book was pocket-sized, with pictures and descriptions of the plants and animals of the Northwest. Dave had given it to me the night before I left. I had put it in the pocket, planning to glance through it during the trip. I pulled it—and the plane ticket—out of the pocket.

The plane stopped and people stood to reach under seats and up on the overhead rack to retrieve their carry-on belongings. I pulled down the bright blue jacket and stuffed my plane ticket and the book in the side pocket. Remembering the brownie, I took it from my shirt and buttoned it in the pocket, too.

As I started down the steps of the plane, the fresh, cool air, with its unfamiliar forest scent, made me feel a surge of excitement. This trip might be more fun than I had thought it would be!

Inside the one-story white terminal building, I felt a little nervous as I approached the group of people that already had started to wave and shout greetings at the passengers straggling in a line from the plane. Dad had to work the last day so he'd asked one of the pilots from the air service to meet me and fly me out to New River.

The crowd was slowly thinning as I walked toward it. Clumps of people talking excitedly were walking together toward the baggage area. How do you spot a pilot you've never seen? I stopped and was looking slowly over the faces when a small woman with graying hair in a long braid walked toward me. "Lisa Gallagher?" she asked. The dark blue eyes in the weathered face were steady.

"Yes."

"Your father said I'd recognize you by the tan, the long blond hair, and the throwing arm," she said. "I'm Martha Allison, your pilot." Her grin was open and friendly. As she took my arm, I could feel the strength in her small hand. "Let's go get your baggage and I'll give you the same speech I give everybody else who flies with M&R Air Service for the first time."

She talked as we walked through the terminal, "First, there are only seven other bush pilots in the state that have more air time than I do. One of them is my husband."

We stopped in the baggage area, and she continued, "We're famous for running one of the safest charters around. People who crash in one of our planes don't make good customers."

I laughed. "Crashing is not one of my ambitions."

We picked up my pack from the baggage area and walked out to the parking lot, where we got in the battered company pickup truck to make the trip to the bay, where the charter plane was kept.

Chapter Two

After a drive of about a half hour, we turned on a narrow road. It led down to the huge bay that had been visible through the tall trees since we had left the airport. When we slowed to come into the clearing by the water, I was surprised to see so many planes. They were sitting out there in the water, tethered to buoys, looking like so many awkward ducks bobbing in the choppy little waves.

"Is this part of the airport?" I asked.

Martha laughed. "No, you'll find planes all over the place up here. It's the best way to get around. Sometimes the *only* way. For instance, you can't *drive* to Juneau. It's a choice between boat and air."

I must have looked surprised, because she continued, "Yes, we're the only state capital without a road leading to it. In the winter that can be quite a problem. Last January a parts salesman dropped by to see us on his way to Anchorage. He'd planned to be in Juneau only half a day. But the weather closed in, and he left eleven days later by boat."

Martha braked the pickup to a stop near a weatherbeaten building that seemed to half office and half garage. "And here, Lisa, are the official quarters of M&R Air Service. The M you've met, and the R is for my husband Ralph." She pointed up at the small, hand-lettered sign that hung over the doorway. "The reason it's M&R and not R&M is because we cut a deck of cards to see whose initial would go first, and I high-carded him!" She grinned, remembering it.

"How soon will we be ready to go?" I asked.

"We're all set up. The plane is loaded and checked out, so all we have to do is file a flight plan and check the weather."

I thought of how bumpy it had been as we flew into Juneau on the big plane. I said, "I understand weather can be a problem up here."

Martha nodded, opening the door to the office, "Yeah, weather up here can be more than just a problem. The changes can be faster and the storms trickier than in most places. That's why we're more cautious."

While she was making phone calls inside the building, I wandered around outside to look things over. Not far from the water were three gas pumps and a shed that seemed to be for repairing planes. I saw men that looked like mechanics going in and out of it. Again, I couldn't help but compare the place to Los Angeles International Airport, where uniformed employees took care of everything and things moved with computer precision. This place seemed like something out of the past.

The glacier that Martha had told me about on

the way to the bay was visible to the east; mountains towered over the city. Everything human seemed small and ramshackle next to the immensity of nature. I didn't feel protected the way I did in Los Angeles. What if the weather *does* get nasty, I thought.

Martha appeared and interrupted my thoughts. "I've checked the weather," she said, as she came out of the office. "We'll have to keep an eye on a cold front, but it shouldn't be a problem. I'll look over the plane one more time, and then we're on our way." We walked together down to a silver seaplane tied to the floating wharf. As I stepped out on the wharf, I could feel it move under my feet, and excitement surged through me. An adventure, I thought.

"Climb in," Martha said, hoisting herself easily up and into the pilot's seat. I stepped on the plane's right pontoon, as I had seen her do; it gave under my weight. "It won't tip over," said Martha. I put my other foot on the step and pulled myself into the plane beside her. There was a smell of oil and gas and salt air.

Martha checked the dials and indicators to satisfy herself that everything was ready.

I looked at my watch. "Will we be in New River by dark?" I asked. I was apprehensive about flying through the dark in a small plane, particularly over those mountains.

"Easy," she answered. "The sun doesn't set this far north until almost ten, so we have lots of time. I have to make one stop at a place called Kake to drop off some parts, then we'll head for New River. Are you ready?"

"Ready," I answered.

She reached across me to slam the door and slid the plane window open. "Clear!" she shouted, cranking the engine into life.

As we droned our way into Kake, Martha talked about her experiences flying in the wilderness, and I regained my enthusiasm and sense of adventure. When we landed, two men were waiting for us on a dock. They unloaded the boxes of parts from the cargo compartment.

Two packages were left back behind the seats. "Shouldn't that stuff back there go, too?" I asked.

Martha glanced over the back of her seat. "No," she said. "Those are parachutes."

"Parachutes?"

"We always carry them out here," said Martha, as she started up the engine. "But I've never used one yet. I *have* used the survival packs attached to them, though." She looked at me out of the corner of her eye.

"You *have*?"

She laughed. "Sometimes when the weather gets bad, I land on a lake or river to wait it out. When that happens, I'll sometimes get out the fishing gear in the survival pack and sit on the pontoon to fish. There's not much else to do."

"Do you have to do that often?"

"Often enough. I stay on the right side of caution. I always figure cargo can wait."

"And you've never used a parachute?"

"Never," she said, as the plane came up off the water and into the air. "Not in twenty-five years of flying. But if I had to use one, that's the kind I'd want. The nice thing about that chute is that it goes on just like a jacket and you can tie things to the leg straps, everything up to the kitchen sink. Some of the smoke jumpers use this kind of chute, and they carry two, three-hundred pounds of equipment with them."

On the way down to Kake, the plane had flown over low mountains, ocean bays, and islands. Now, as we headed inland, we left the ocean behind, and I watched the mountains grow higher and more rugged through patches of clouds. Then the mountains ahead began to lose themselves in the overcast. Martha pointed off to our right. "See those clouds over there that look so nice and fluffy? They're thunderheads from that cold front. They can really throw a plane around."

I was surprised to see one of the thunderheads glow with lightning for an instant. Martha saw it, too. "We don't find too many storms like that close to the coast, but when we do, we give them a wide berth. That cold front has really stirred things up, but we'll try to go around it."

As we flew on through the afternoon sky, the droning engine and the long day made my eyelids heavy. Our conversation died into silence, and it was almost a half-hour later when Martha banked the plane to turn us back to our original heading. "See that solid white blanket down there?" she said, pointing to a layer of clouds below us. "That's what the weather report called patchy clouds."

"How can we see to land through that?" I wondered out loud.

"We can't," said Martha. "We're still a long way from New River. I had to go way off course to duck that weather. By the time we get over the mountains and back down to where we want to be, we should be out of the clouds."

I nodded at her answer and went back to my half-doze, coming up out of it from time to time to see if there was a break in the clouds. But the weather seemed to get worse, not better. Although Martha climbed to escape the clouds, they kept getting thicker and higher until finally they reached up and close in around us. Rain began to spatter on the windshield, and the small plane was shoved up and down in the gusty wind currents.

After almost an hour of flying in a turbulent, all-grey world, Martha took the radio's earphones and mike off the clip that held them to the instrument panel and said to me, "We should have broken out of this twenty minutes ago. I'll call Juneau and find out what they can tell us."

Slipping on the earphones, she spoke into the mike again and again without an answer. Finally, she took the earphones off and snapped them, with the mike, back on the hook. "Lisa, I'm afraid you're going to have to put off your backpacking trip for a day. With those thunderheads, all I can get on the radio is static. This storm has pushed us far enough off course that the safest thing for us to do is to turn around and hightail it back to the coast."

As she spoke, she guided the lurching airplane into a half circle. "I figure we're way south of Juneau, so we'll head west to get out of this stuff. Sorry about the change in plans."

I answered quickly, "Right now, I'd be glad to get anywhere that's not moving." My stomach was beginning to react to the rollercoaster ride the storm was giving us.

We had flown only for a little while on the new heading when Martha cocked her head to listen to the sound of the engine.

"Something wrong?" I asked.

"I don't know," she answered, her eyes scanning the instrument panel. "I thought I heard something strange in the engine."

Then I heard it, too. The engine was changing from its steady drone to a chugging like that of a washing machine. Martha quickly throttled back, her eyes riveted to the gauges. Our speed decreased. I wondered what Martha was thinking, but she said nothing. Again she tried the radio, as she decreased the speed of the engine even further. Nothing. Nervousness made my voice edgy. "Did you get Juneau?" I asked.

"No," said Martha shortly, as she went on studying the dials and gauges and nursing the engine. When she spoke again, her voice showed strain. "I think it's a rod bearing. If we can just keep oil pressure, we can limp on in."

We jolted on through the dark grey sky. Martha kept pulling back on the throttle to run the engine slower and slower, her eyes intent on the instrument panel, but the sound of the chugging engine became rougher and rougher. Finally Martha turned to me and studied my face for a moment before she said, "I want you to climb into the back seat and buckle in next to your pack."

"Why? What's going to happen?" I felt fear twisting in the pit of my stomach.

"It's all right, Lisa." Her voice was steady. "We're in a bit of a spot, but we can handle it. Now, please do what I asked." Her last statement was a command. I was really frightened. I wanted to shout, "No!" or "Take me home!" or "I can't!" but her blue eyes held me as she continued,

"You're going to have to hold on because we're bouncing quite a bit."

I turned to look at the back seat. It seemed far away. I couldn't imagine how I'd be able to climb back there.

"Do it now, Lisa." Her voice was firm. I unsnapped my belt. Holding onto the seat back, I started to crawl over. The plane lurched, and I felt myself falling sideways. The same strong hand that had greeted me at the airport now grabbed my jacket and helped me to steady myself. I forced myself to keep going. Grabbing the belt that held my pack, I pulled myself over the back of the seat just as the next gust hit. It knocked me back toward the windshield, but my grip held. I twisted to sit next to my pack. My hands fumbled at the seat belt, trying to get it fastened before the next buffet of wind. I made it.

Martha looked back. "How are you doing?"

"Okay, I guess." My voice sounded strange to my ears.

She listened to the engine for a moment, then she spoke again. "Just to be on the safe side, let's get those chutes out. Unsnap the one closer to you and hand it up to me. Be careful. Don't pull the D-ring or it will open."

The fear I had pushed down in my mind rushed through my body again, but I turned and forced my hand back to the belt to pop it loose. The plane gave a sudden lurch and pitched the parachute forward. All I could do was get out of its way. Martha guided it to the seat beside her and buckled it in.

"You're doing fine, Lisa," she said. "How do you feel?"

I swallowed to try to ease the tightness of my

throat before I said, "All right, I think." My voice was a squeak.

"Good," she replied. "Now reach back and get the other chute and put it on. But don't fasten the leg straps."

I tugged the second parachute toward me. With the survival pack tied on below, it was awkward, but I finally was able to haul it up. I put my arms through the straps. When I finished, Martha reached back and checked the tightness of the harness. Then she reached down and pulled the leg straps free so that the ends were loose. She said, "Now if anything happens, just pull your pack over to you and put the leg straps through the pack straps. Then snap the leg straps in place. Okay?"

I wasn't sure what she meant. It seemed complicated. As I opened my mouth to ask, the engine made a grinding noise and began to vibrate. Martha quickly closed the throttle. The engine was barely running now. I noticed several smears of black smoke streaking past the window.

Martha looked back and forth from the engine to me. Then, in a strained, urgent voice, she said, "Go ahead and put the leg straps through the pack straps."

I fumbled frantically for the seat belt that held my pack in. I found the release, pushed it, and felt the pack give with the swaying of the plane. Suddenly a bright flash of flame burst from the engine. Martha's hands darted over the instrument panel as she flipped switches. White foam from the fire extinguisher spattered on the windshield as the engine died. She spun around to look at me. "Is your pack attached to the leg straps?" I stared at her. I couldn't move. I couldn't speak.

She heaved herself halfway over the seat back and with expert hands snapped the pack in place. Her voice seemed loud now that the engine was dead. The silence was terrifying. "Keep your hand on the D-ring right here. Don't pull until you're out the door, then pull hard." In a quieter voice, she asked, "Do you understand?"

My mouth worked but no sound came out.

"There's no time," Martha said. "In just a few seconds this plane could be a flaming coffin. Now get ready."

She leaned over to the far door and jerked at the latches. The door fell away. The rush of cold air made me gasp. The whole left side of the cockpit seemed to be empty space.

Martha turned back to me again. "Unsnap your seat belt." I did as she said. "Good luck, Lisa." Her hands half-lifted and half-shoved me toward the open door. "Now!" I closed my eyes and tried to send strength to my rubbery legs. There was a lurch of the plane, a blast of cold air, and I felt myself falling.

Blind panic engulfed me. I opened my eyes to see the wheel of the plane pass my shoulder. I grabbed for it, but I missed. My eyes shut again. I was falling faster, it seemed. Terror paralyzed me. Then, almost like another person, a part of my mind fought back. "Pull the ring!" I shouted to myself. My hand dug frantically between the pack and my body. I grabbed the D-ring and pulled. I felt it give and thought, "I've broken it."

Something flapped and cracked behind me. Then giant hands jerked me to a teeth-rattling halt. It was as if time had stopped. No noise. No rush of cold air. I opened my eyes and looked up. The billowy white parachute seemed to cover the grey sky. Relief flooded through me.

"I made it! I made it!" The sound of my voice filled my ears. Then I felt the pain of the leg straps biting into my legs from the weight of the pack. I reached down and lifted the pack up.

I floated in the air, slowly drifting down toward the ground. It was strangely peaceful. A brief thought of the plane: I looked but couldn't see it anywhere. Martha would parachute out of the plane, too, and we would find each other on the ground. The ground! What would I do when I came down? I looked below to see a plain of green treetops. I would land in *them*. Then the treetops seemed to rush up toward me.. A branch slapped against my leg, then another and another. I buried my face in my arms as I plunged through the branches. Suddenly, I jerked to a stop. I tried to peer through the branches to see how high off the ground I was. What if I were fifty feet up? How would I get to the ground? What if the parachute should come free and drop me? I grabbed the nearest tree limb and pushed the smaller branches aside to look down. The ground, strewn with pine needles, was less than three feet below my boots.

Chapter Three

At first I didn't move, but just hung paralyzed in the tree, like someone in a straitjacket caught in an elevator between floors. Where was Martha? I knew I must have looked silly, hanging there. I kicked my legs, and felt sillier. It was quiet. I could hear the soft sound of rain all around me. No Martha. No sound of Martha. No sound of an airplane either. It was as if I had dropped down out of nowhere. I started to fumble with the hook of the parachute, hoping I could get loose and down out of the tree. The snap was hard to reach, and it took some time before I felt it release. Too late, I remembered that it was the harness that held my pack. I grabbed the straps just before the pack fell free and eased it down as close to the ground as I could before letting it drop. It hit softly.

The sides of the harness were still fastened. I tried again and again to loosen them, but my weight held them tight. As I struggled, rain water cascaded from the tree branches onto my head. Still no luck. I let myself hang in the harness as I thought. Then the heavy branches of the tree gave me an idea—I'd swing over to a branch and climb high enough to get my weight off the harness. Tarzan of the Northwest, I thought. From my dead-still position, I rocked myself back and forth to start myself swinging. It didn't work. I kept trying, but nothing happened. Finally, angry and frustrated, I grabbed the risers of the parachute and jerked furiously. It gave a little, and I slipped down a few inches. I jerked even harder. Without warning, the parachute pulled free, and I tumbled to the ground below.

Damp from the drizzling rain, the parachute fell over me like a collapsing tent. I pawed my way out from under, suppressing a sudden, wild desire to laugh. I unhooked the harness, shook myself free, stood up, and looked around. A thick wall of pine and spruce made it difficult for me to see more than a few yards. Little pools of rainwater lay in hollows filled with pine needles.

It seemed very quiet. Like most city people, I was used to being surrounded by noises I didn't consciously hear: trucks on the freeway, radios, stereos, kids screaming, the hum of electrical appliances. I missed those noises. I said to myself, give me noise pollution—*lots* of it. Standing there, somewhere in the middle of what had been a huge expanse on the map, I felt like a mere dot on the topography.

Martha should be down by now, I thought. How would she know where I was? I cupped my hands to my mouth and shouted, "Here! Over here!" as loud as I could. The noise died away in the forest, and the silence returned. Nothing. No reply. Just the soft sound of rain falling all about me.

Through my mind flashed the memory of the last few frantic moments aboard the plane and the terrifying feeling of falling through space. I listened, hoping to hear a plane or Martha's shout. Then—a noise! "Here! Over here, Martha!" The sound of my shout frightened the bird—a crow—that had made the noise, and it flew away, cawing excitedly.

What time was it? I looked at my watch, which had been battered in my frantic attempt to get out of the tree but was still ticking—five o'clock. Martha had said it didn't get dark here until almost ten. That gave her five hours to get down and find me. If she had managed to make radio contact, it would mean five hours for rescue planes to search. I decided to keep calling her every ten minutes so she wouldn't miss me in the thick forest. I've got to let her know where I am, I thought. Again, I listened, and thought I heard a plane. It was the sound of my own blood drumming in my ears.

A drop of water fell on my face, and I realized my hair was soaked. I wrung out the ends by twisting them in my hands like a towel, then I sat down and pulled a piece of the parachute over my head, like a lady in a January rainstorm using a newspaper as an umbrella. Inside my waterproof jacket, the rest of me was relatively dry.

"Well," I said to myself. "You're in the wilderness, Lisa." The conversational tone of my own voice startled me at first. Then I decided I liked it; it was company. I continued: "You'd laugh your head off, Kyle, if you could see me out here."

A scene went through my mind: I am rescued by a helicopter, and hours later I land at Los Angeles International Airport, where reporters are waiting to interview me. I am the first one down the ramp.

The flashbulbs of the photographers almost blind me. When I reach the ground, reporters surround me, shouting questions. From the corner of my eye, I see Kyle watching me, admiringly. He tries to push through the crowd .... But I was in the forest, not in L.A., nowhere near L.A.

Again I stood up and yelled for Martha, shouting into the quiet, and again, there was only the sound of rain, in answer, mocking me. Finally, my throat sore, I rested my back against the tree that had caught me. Where *was* she?

I wished I could see the sky. Maybe I could climb a tree or something, then I might be able to see where the plane had crashed, if it did crash. But a flaming plane could start a forest fire. Maybe Martha didn't make it; maybe she went down with the plane. Such things *did* happen in real life. They didn't only happen in disaster movies. I pushed the thought away.

I remembered reading about how rescue planes combed an area, back and forth. Would they be able to see me? The treetops formed a thick blanket between me and the sky, where everything important had happened and would happen. It was from that invisible sky that rescue would come. I wanted to see it. Again I wondered if Martha had been able to do something with the radio so rescuers would know where we were. The forest was so large, and we had been off course. I thought: I wish a plane would come and fly me out *right now*.

It was seven o'clock before I decided that it was likely nothing would happen that night. I said, out loud, "If I'm going to spend the night here, I better get organized." Saying it made me feel better. I dug in the pack, found the flashlight I had packed, pulled it out, clicked it on once to check the batteries, turned it off, and stuck it in my jacket pocket.

Then I noticed that the ground sloped away under my feet. Downhill. I remembered something Dave had said when we were talking about backpacking and how people sometimes got lost. "If people would just head downhill when they think they're lost, they'd be better off." But I wasn't lost. And the best thing for me to do would be to wait where I was.

Before I unpacked, I'd have to find a good place to sleep. The spot where I was sloped too much—I needed level ground. I hated to leave the tree I had landed in because it was familiar. I bundled up the parachute and tied it with its own straps. Putting on the pack and half-carrying, half-dragging the chute and survival kit, I made my way down the sloping ground through the trees. After a while, I stopped and listened. There was another sound over the sound of the rain—a heavier water sound. Slowly, I pushed through branches of smaller trees, following the sound. The ground began to flatten out, and I broke through the underbrush into a small clearing with a stream running through it. About ten yards from where I stood, there was a flat area under a large tree. I walked down to it, stumbling with the awkward bundle of parachute. Once there, I dropped the chute, and swung the pack from my shoulders, and then went over and looked at the stream tumbling over the rocks. I put my hand in—the water felt icy cold.

Water. At home it came from the tap—from the Colorado River down through aqueducts and purifying plants, through pipes, to the faucet. The

Sparkletts bottle, which sat on its stand in the kitchen, contained pure spring water, from somewhere in the mountains. All safe to drink. Certified. Advertised. What about this water? I knew that campers sometimes boiled stream water to purify it, but the woods was too wet—I'd never be able to find enough dry wood to start a fire. Then I laughed. Here I was, miles into the wilderness, a pinpoint on that map, worrying about clean water. It's people who pollute, I thought. I knelt by the stream and cupped some of the cold water in my hands. I drank. Then I sat down on the bank.

I liked being near the water. This wasn't the Pacific, but it was a good substitute, a focus, a place to be among all those look-alike trees. I thought about how in the summer, at home, I was usually a beach bum—I'd spend all day down near the boardwalk in Venice, getting a tan and bodysurfing. I'd offered to teach Dave to body-surf earlier, in the spring. He had said, "I'd like that. In return, I'll take you camping."

Teaching Dave turned out to be fun—he was a willing, apt pupil. The first time he tried to catch a wave, he took it too late—the gathering crest broke over him and rolled him. He came up sputtering and laughing. "You didn't tell me about *that*!" he shouted. "I couldn't tell which way was up down there. Or if I'd come up at all!" But he hadn't stopped trying, and when he did catch his first wave and rode it in to shore, he had jumped up and waved his arms in victory. I had known he was hooked.

A sound in the bush broke into my thoughts. What am I doing here? I thought, feeling suddenly panicked. I looked at my watch. It was 8:10, time to call for Martha again. I tried, but I was no longer expecting to hear an answer. I thought that she might have decided to wait until morning to search for me. Perhaps she was somewhere near me in the trees, bedding down for the night.

I wanted someone to talk to, or even a radio—some sound of civilization, a voice, not just the sounds of the rain and the running stream. The quiet made me nervous. I tried singing, but the sound of my voice was thin in the wilderness, and the words seemed silly. Who's going to hear me? I thought. My voice faded away, and the silence came surging in on me again.

To keep myself busy, I took stock of what I had with me. I wished I had a light tent, the kind Dave had shown me in the sporting goods store. Then the parachute gave me an idea. I felt the cloth—it seemed slick enough to keep water off. I tugged at the bundle and tried to spread the parachute out under the tree. It was a confusing mass of fabric and lines. Finally I got hold of one of the edges. Taking the attached lines, I pulled the edge of the parachute over the lowest branch of the tree. One at a time, working carefully, I attached six of the lines along the branch, then, pulling and tugging, I stretched the rest out as a makeshift tent. Taking my pack and the survival kit, I got in under the tent. I untied the sleeping bag from the pack and laid it out behind me. Then I took out all my belongings from the pack and spread them out: the flashlight, my clothes, my wallet, makeup kit, toothbrush, toothpaste, soap, comb, hairbrush, packs of tissues, poncho—all the things that I had packed so carefully that morning. The morning seemed so far away. I undid the straps that held the survival kit to the parachute harness, opened the flap, and sorted the contents. There were eight fish hooks, heavy fishing lines, a first-aid kit, insect repellent (which I put on), a box of wooden matches, a pot with a bail handle, a hunting knife, some wire in a plastic pouch labeled "Animal Snares"—and food! At the bottom were foil pouches of dehydrated food like the ones I had seen in the sporting goods store. It might be a cold, wet, and lonely night, but at least it wouldn't be a hungry one.

What else? I reached into my pocket and took out the brownie, wrapped in a napkin with "*Western Airlines*" imprinted on the corner. I put the brownie, napkin under it, on the sleeping bag, too. Then I added to it the book Dave had give me, my wallet, and the plane ticket, which had also been in my jacket pocket. My collection, laid out like a picnic lunch. All the colors of civilization laying on the lumpy surface of the khaki sleeping bag in the middle of a vast brown-and-green wilderness. The colors made the world outside the forest seem more real to me. I thought of eating the brownie. Chocolate, nuts, flour. Baking companies. Trucks, airline stewardesses. About 250 calories. I didn't care about the calories. My hunger was there, but I didn't really feel like eating. I packed everything up again, and sat under the parachute on the damp ground.

It was almost nine o'clock. By now my father would really be worried about me. I wondered what he had done. He had probably talked to Martha's husband, called the Juneau airport to see if we had taken off. Had he called my mother yet? My mind went to the living room of the apartment, to the green phone by the couch, to my mother sitting there, a look of strain and worry on her face, talking into the mouthpiece.

Where was Martha? What would I do if nobody ever came? I had read somewhere that if your plane goes down in a wilderness, it's best to stay where you are so rescue teams can find you. It saves energy. If you start walking, you're likely to go in circles. I thought about starting a fire as a signal for the search planes. It was too wet. Perhaps, I thought, it will be drier tomorrow and I can start a tree on fire so the helicopters will see it.... But that might start a forest fire...

The light was beginning to fade. I took the brownie from the pocket of my jacket and slowly ate it, thinking it might be my last piece of chocolate, then decided that I was being too dramatic. B.J. liked to say that I was lucky to be able to eat chocolate without getting zits. Instead of sitting on the wet ground, I would have given anything to be pulled up in a chair at a formica-topped table at Zacky's, eating a cheeseburger and french fries. I'd even have settled for the school cafeteria and their awful Friday spaghetti. Or that half sandwich I had left at lunch.

It was getting darker. I unzipped the sleeping bag, then I took off my boots and stuck them in a corner of the tent so they would dry off some during the night. I pulled my comb out of my pack and combed my hair so it wouldn't look too messy when the helicopters landed. As I started to climb into the sleeping bag, I noticed how damp my clothes were, even my shirt, which had been covered by the jacket. I knew that if I got the bag wet, I would be cold all night, so I pulled off my clothes and put them over by my boots. It felt strange to be naked in the woods, but there was no one to see me, and I was soon zipped into the sleeping bag. The cloth of the sleeping bag felt good against my skin.

Something rustled in the underbrush. Fear started up in the back of my mind and I tried to push it back. What was it? The sound stopped, and my mind searched for explanations. I remembered Dave saying that almost every animal in the woods was afraid of humans, so there was no reason for humans to be scared of them. It was easier to say this than to feel it. Dave had also said that the woods was like a painting. You learn to see more things in it the longer you look at it and the better you know it: animal trails, changes in the colors of plants and trees. "Do you know how many colors of green there are in a forest?" he had asked. "You should try to count them sometime." Then he had talked of night noises. "You can hear animals rustling around. It's a different world at night. After a while, you start to feel as though you're part of it."

Not true, I thought, then said out loud, "I don't feel part of this at all!" I wanted to be home, watching television or talking on the phone to B.J., not here in the middle of nowhere. I tried pretending Dave was there, but it didn't work. Then I thought about Kyle. What did he know about the woods? Nothing. All he knew were cars and streets and girls. He liked engines, and couldn't care less about nature. Kyle didn't even care much for the beach; he thought it was boring. I tried to remember Kyle's face. I could think of descriptions for parts of it: "dark eyes," "long nose," "beginning of a beard," but the parts wouldn't come together in a picture in my mind. All I could see were the pine needles making a texture of the forest floor and the stream moving, flowing on its way somewhere.

The night closed around me. With the heavy overcast, the thick trees, and the rain, the darkness seemed oppressive. At first I found it hard to go to sleep. I missed the hum of the cars from the San Diego Freeway, the dim light from the streetlights outside my bedroom window, the thumping of the refrigerator (my mother was always saying she'd get it fixed, but she never had).... Then I heard the rustling again. I told myself that something was alive out there, keeping me company, but the thought didn't calm me. A black curtain of darkness was before my eyes, and no matter how I strained, I couldn't see through it. I turned on the flashlight. Its beam pierced the darkness, making eerie shadows of the twigs. I saw nothing unusual in its light, so I turned it off. There was little sound in the wet stillness—only the rain dripping from the trees and the stream whispering along. I heard no planes. The luminous hands on my watch told me that it was 11:15. And that was the last I remembered that night.

Chapter Four

I woke to dim light filtering down through the translucent white cloth of the parachute above my head and remembered immediately where I was and what had happened. Still in the sleeping bag, I sat up and looked around, half-expecting to see a circle of rescuers' faces grinning down at me. But no one was there. The fissured trunk of an old tree, a forest floor thick with pine needles, and some low-growing shrubs were all I saw.

Perhaps Martha is asleep somewhere near, I thought. Loudly, I called her name. Maybe the sound of my voice would wake her up. Then she'd come and tell me that she'd been able to raise Juneau on the radio before she went down. She'd say that the planes were on their way. We'd celebrate by starting a little fire and making breakfast while we exchanged experiences. . . .

No answer. I called again, but the sound of my voice lost itself in the trees and nothing came back. Feeling alone, I took refuge in my usual morning fantasy: my head on Kyle's shoulder, his arm around me, as we sat in his car parked at the top of Topanga Canyon, on the last curve before the road winds down to the Pacific. Feeling Kyle breathe against me, seeing his long-nosed profile, I move closer. A strand of his silky hair brushes my face as he leans toward me. . . . Try as I would, I couldn't get into it.

Back in the real world of the wilderness, I noticed that the rain had stopped. To fight the silence, I spoke aloud, "Hello," I said, to nothing in particular. The sound of my voice startled me. But I continued talking because it was somehow comforting. "I should get up."

My voice cracked. "I really should get up," I continued, as I reached down to feel my clothes. They were still damp. I didn't want to get up. Why couldn't I just close my eyes, and when I opened them again, be lying in my own bed, in my own room, looking up at the white plaster ceiling and trying to decide if I'd spend the day at the beach body-surfing or hacking around with B.J.? "Stop it, Lisa," I told myself. "There are things to do." The decisiveness in my voice encouraged me. I started moving, not quite sure what the "things to do" were. The rasping noise of the metal teeth of the sleeping bag zipper unzipping sounded strange. It was so different from the sounds the wind and water made that it seemed jarring and unnatural.

When I stood, the condensation on the inside of the parachute cascaded down on my head. The cold morning air made me shiver, so I hunted quickly through my pack for dry clothes—a warm flannel shirt, heavy Levi's, and wool socks. Dressed, I pulled on and tied up the still damp boots. The activity made me feel better. This time when I called Martha, the answering silence did not disappoint me so much.

What to do now? At home, the first thing on my agenda when I got up was a nice hot shower. I would go into the blue-tiled bathroom, turn on the water in the shower, adjusting it to just the right temperature, step in, and let the water fall over me. My "apartment" here was the space that had become my camp, where huge tree branches curved protectively over the parachute tent. No blue-tiled bathroom, no hot water, no thick towels.

At home, when Mother and I had one of our infrequent spats, I'd sometimes lock myself in the bathroom. But here, there was no door to lock. How do you lock a forest? Look at you! I said to myself, feeling a smile come over my face—you're getting nostalgic for a bathroom!

Besides, there is a solution to the hot water problem, I told myself, sitting down next to the pack to look for the bail-handled pot. Hot water is water that is hot. Water from the stream, "hot" from a fire. Dead branches plus a match from the survival pack equals fire. Easy. At least I could wash my face in water from the stream heated over the fire, then maybe cook some breakfast. Yes, responded my empty stomach. After that, it would be full morning, and the search planes would be coming, so I could pile a lot of branches on to make a signal fire.

"Yes, a signal fire, just what we need," I said out loud to myself. My voice sounded positive, almost jaunty. "But first a drink of fresh mountain stream water, just like the Sparkletts' ads say." With the bail-handled pot in hand, I walked down to the stream. I filled it where the water splashed noisily over a large rock. The water was so cold that it made my teeth hurt when I drank it, but it tasted good. Sweet water. The phrase came into my mind from somewhere . . . some book I had read about a wagon train going west. The pioneers had been almost dead from thirst when they found a stream of sweet water. All the other drinking pools had been filled with alkali.

At least here there was plenty of water. In the desert, water would be a big problem. It was lucky we hadn't planned on camping in the Mohave.

After I filled the pot again, I took it back to camp, then went to look for firewood. At first it looked easy—dead branches littered the ground. But as I picked up first one twig and then another, they felt heavy and I realized that they were still water-soaked.

Dave had said something about firewood. What was it? My memory shuffled through events and found us sitting on the grass in the park, Dave talking, me only half-listening. He was saying that even after rain, some of the lower branches of spruce and fir are dry, particularly the dead ones, dry enough to burn.

Deciding to check out what he had told me, I walked over to the closest tree and ducked under the lower branches close to the trunk. There! Dead branches, some with dried brown clusters of needles still on them. Only the top was damp, and many of the twigs were dry. Within a half hour, back at my camp I had an impressive pile of firewood and a nice collection of scratches on my hands and arms from the effort. That day on the grass Dave had gone on to tell me never to build a fire on pine needles because it could spread. It was beginning to dawn on me how much information Dave had given me about the woods in the couple of weeks before I left. Every time we were together, he'd tell me something I'd casually listen to then and strained to remember now.

I followed his weeks' old instructions: with my boot heel, I scraped the needles back until I had a large, circular bare spot for a fire. Starting with twigs, I built up a crisscrossed mound of dead wood. I took one of the matches from the survival kit, knelt down, and struck it on a dry piece of wood. As the flame flared, I poked it gently under the twigs. First one twig, then several, burst into flame. With a feeling of satisfaction, I sat back and watched as the yellow tongues of fire licked the wood. Sparks started to jump toward the sky. The wood popped. With alarm, I remembered that trees burn, too. Would the fire reach the tree branches above me? Carefully I reached over and took out a couple of the branches that had not caught on fire yet.

When the fire had begun to die down, I put the pot over it until the water was warm, then poured some into my cupped hand to wash my face. I was trying to choose one of the foil-wrapped packages for breakfast—beef stew or chicken fricassee?—when a noise made me freeze. The low hum was far away but I recognized it immediately—a plane!

Jumping up and waving my arms, I shouted wildly, "Over here! Over here!" before I realized that the pilot could not see or hear me. In a frenzy I piled wood on the fire. The flames leaped higher. It wasn't flame I wanted, but smoke. More wood? Damp wood? Frantically, I grabbed up handfuls of pine needles and threw them on the fire. The puff of white smoke was encouraging. I leaned over and scooped up more, threw them on. I didn't care if the whole forest went up in flames if I was found.

I paused for an instant to listen. The sound was fainter now. I didn't want to believe it. Jumping up and down, I screamed at the patches of dull gray sky I could see far above me. "Over here! I'm over here! Listen, hey, I'm over *here*!" But I was trapped under the thick cover of tree tops, no more visible to the pilot of the plane than an ant in a field of hay.

I stopped calling to listen. All I could hear was the crackling of the fire and my labored breathing. I ran a few yards into the trees to get away from the noise of the fire and tried to hold my breath. My ears strained to hear an engine hum. Nothing.

Disappointment brought tears to my eyes, then I started to sob. I stood there, my mouth trying to shape the words for one last shout through the tears. It was useless. Breathing heavily from crying, I turned and walked back to the fire. A gentle breeze stirred the tree branches, making a kind of moaning. I jerked around to listen. Nothing. It was nothing.

Several times I swallowed to stop the tears, then spoke aloud again. "They're looking for me. That plane proves it. It's just a matter of time until I'm found. I'll just take it easy and keep the fire going." I took a deep breath that came in jerks, then said to that other part of myself, the part that was terrified, "Just don't get all worked up. It's just a matter of time." The terrified voice whimpered in my head, "But how do I know that plane was looking for me? Who am I to think every plane that flies overhead is looking for Lisa Gallagher? It could be a mail plane or something, maybe a rich hunter being flown into the wilds on a charter."

Frustrated, I shouted, "Oh, be quiet!" to my own mind. I really *was* talking to myself. It meant I was scared and alone, that was all. I thought of Kyle's experience when he had visited a psychologist, who asked him to sit on a stool and be one part of himself talking to another, "pretend" Kyle on another stool. When Kyle objected, saying only crazy people talked to themselves, the psychologist had replied that all people have several voices. Kyle still hadn't liked it much, but he had had no choice. His parents, worried because he was sullen most of the time and failing in school, had given him an ultimatum—psychologist or private school, *military* school. The shrink was the better deal, he said. I was afraid for him, knowing how his emotions fouled him up. "He's just a spoiled brat," B.J. had said, but B.J. wasn't exactly noted for her sympathy.

I let my mind wander through various scenes with Kyle for a while. It gave me some comfort, as I sat by my ebbing fire recovering from crying. At last I realized again I was hungry, so I mixed some dried stew into the rest of the water and put the pot back on the glowing fire. The food in my stomach calmed me down even more, and I began to think about how I would look when the rescuers came. I was sure I looked a mess—tear-streaked, soot-streaked, hair in snarls. The face wash of an hour earlier had been done in by my crying jag. Gathering up soap, toothpaste, and a toothbrush, I went to the stream, dipped the brush into the water, squeezed paste on it, and, kneeling there, brushed my teeth. I spat into the stream as I did into the basin at home and watched the white foam float down the current of fast-moving water. It's going to the ocean, I thought idly.

Back at camp, I combed my hair. There were pine needles caught in it, so it took quite a while, and when I was done, the comb was full of tangled blond hairs. Looking at myself in the makeup mirror as I put on lipstick, I thought I didn't look too bad. My eyes were a little puffy from crying, that was all.

All that morning and late into the afternoon, I listened for another plane. Whether I was fixing food from the survival pack (chicken soup) or hunting more firewood or reading Dave's book on plants and animals, it was always with at least part of my mind focused on the sounds around me trying to hear that distant drone again. It was like being at home, bored yet nervous, waiting for Kyle to call, knowing he wouldn't. The sight of those tree tops was as frustrating as the sight of a silent phone, stubbornly refusing to ring.

Sometimes I called for Martha, trying to keep to a schedule of no more than a half hour between shouts. She couldn't get too far in a half hour if she were walking. She'd be certain to be in shouting distance and would hear me.

Four o'clock. I wondered if my poor, battered wristwatch was accurate. I had wound it the night before and it was still ticking. Maybe the fall in the parachute had slowed it down, or maybe I had knocked it against something. Sitting against a tree trunk, I hunched my shoulders, feeling tightness in my back and neck. It made me realize how hard I had been straining to hear the sound of a plane.

I stood, and to loosen up did some warm-up exercises from track—rotated my head, touched my toes. Then I took a few quick steps and heaved an imaginary javelin at the trees.

Four-fifteen. Time was dragging. I thought of home, then of my father, somewhere in Juneau, trying to find out where I was. It was Tuesday. Would Kyle know I was missing? By now, he would probably have heard. My father would have called my mother, who would have called B.J., who would have called someone in the grapevine from school, who would have called Kyle. I retreated into my imagination, where a Hollywood fantasy started to play: Kyle sells his beloved car to pay for a flight to Juneau, where he meets my father, organizes a search party, parachutes into the wilderness to look for me. Realizing he loves me, and not Kathy, he never sleeps, but keeps going, day and night, hoping. . . . Even I couldn't continue this one. My own extravagance made me smile.

Four-thirty. The combination of boredom (nothing to do) and anxiety (when would they come?) made me jumpy. I knew I'd have to do something to keep busy. To sit under the tree and fantasize was ridiculous. Fishing! That would be a way to pass the time. It was what Martha did when she was forced down on a lake. Using the knife from the survival kit, I sawed away at a willow limb; it would serve as a pole. It took some time to hack through the living wood. The resulting cut end was jagged and splintery, but the pole would do, I thought. I attached a piece of heavy fishing line to the pole, and tied a hook on the end of the line. Just like Tom Sawyer, I said to myself, as I surveyed my work—crude, but it should do the job.

Bait? Anything small and alive would be all

right. Down by the stream, I found a bug that might be appetizing to a trout and pushed the hook through it. It made me feel a little nauseous to see it wiggle. I plopped the line into the stream. Almost at once the hook snagged on something on the stream bottom. I pulled at the line, but the hook didn't come free. Impatient, I walked up and down the edge of the stream, holding the taut line at different angles to see if I could unsnag the hook, but I had no luck. Finally, I jerked hard on the pole and the line flew up out of the water. Both bait and hook were lost.

I was trying to decide whether to go back for another hook when I felt a sharp, itching sensation near my elbow and started to scratch it. And another, on one of my fingers. Mosquitoes! They were whining around my head now; they seemed to have come out of nowhere. Dave's book had warned about the mosquitoes in Southeastern Alaska. They came out at dusk, the book said. The reality was worse than the print had promised. These mosquitoes, hungry for blood, were out in force. I was the best blood supply they had found in a long time.

Scratching myself and slapping at the mosquitoes, which stayed in a cloud around my head, I beelined it back to camp and to the bottle of insect repellent in the survival pack. I had forgotten the hook lost on the bottom of the stream. Back at the fire, the smoke kept the mosquitoes off a little while while I searched for and found the plastic bottle and smeared some of the repellent on my face and arms. It seemed to help.

Sitting there, I closed my eyes and tried to pick up any faint sound of rescue. Nothing. I knew it would soon be getting dark, too late for anyone to continue a search. "Tomorrow, I bet they have every plane in the state buzzing around here." I wanted very much to believe that. Then I added, "Before it gets too dark, I better get things straightened up. We want the rescuers to find a neat camp." "If they come," answered a voice in my head. I was reminded of the cartoon devils that sit on the shoulders of characters in comic books. I tried to snuff it.

With everything put away, and a pot boiling on the fire for the cocoa I'd found in the pack, the forest seemd a friendlier place than it had the night before. As I mixed the cocoa, I found myself wondering how many calories it contained and laughed: "I've jumped out of an airplane, gotten plunked down in the middle of nowhere, and I am completely lost. But one thing for sure -- I've got to come out of this thinner."

Later that night, as I snuggled down in the sleeping bag, I thought, "When they find me tomorrow, I'll have to remember to tell them I've discovered a new quick weight-loss plan—The Wilderness Diet."

Chapter Five

On the pack flap was a cluster of five lines plus one—~~IIII~~ |. Six days. Now I began to add another line to make seven days of waiting, listening, hoping. It had been the third day when I had started to make the marks. Just before dark, I'd been sitting by the fire, thinking how I had been in the forest four days, then had realized I was wrong—it had only been three. The mistake scared me. Yet, at first I didn't want to take the pen and do the tally. "Why keep count?" I'd said to myself. "The planes will be here tomorrow for sure. It doesn't make any difference." There was another side to it, though—by keeping track, I would be saying that the days meant something, that rescue would come. I was like someone in jail, writing marks on the concrete wall to keep track of the length of his sentence.

Now, as I rubbed the ballpoint back and forth across the thick fabric, I tried to push the word "week" out of my mind. It seemed to be a longer time than seven days. "They should have been here," I said, my voice sounding annoyed, as if I were talking about a missed appointment or a broken fingernail.

I put the pen away and leaned back against the tree trunk that had become my chair back. What if they didn't come? Always before when that thought had entered my mind, I had denied it with a quick, "Don't be silly. It's just taking them a while is all." I had imagined the pilots of the search planes planning the rescue effort on a map. They would comb the woods, flying back and forth in a grid pattern. It might take some time, but eventually they'd get to the square where I was. But as time went by, I found it harder to imagine, harder to think of a real world out there somewhere beyond my camp. Planes. People on phones and radios. Maps with grids. What I did know was the silence of the forest. Tree trunks like columns. Empty patches of sky.

The question came back, waiting for an answer: *What if they don't come?* Shifting my mind away from it, I considered the last seven days. When I remembered where I was, a tiny human being in that immense expanse of wilderness I'd seen from the air, I was overwhelmed with loneliness. Then I would have given almost anything to hear B.J.'s confidential voice on the phone, to click on a light, to feel one of Mother's quick hugs, to wake up to the smell of coffee, to hear the "hello" of a supermarket clerk. I'd think at such times, "There's nothing to *do*" and I'd want to tear my way out of the trees that seemed to close down around me.

At other times, when I was busily engaged in something—making a fire or fixing up camp—I had not thought of myself at all, had been so involved in what I was doing that I seemed to lose myself in it.

"Maybe I'm not a full-fledged pioneer, but at least I'm getting along all right." I said it with some pride. After all, I had stayed alive. I'd learned a lot. The second night, I'd found a way to keep the mosquitoes off my face while I slept—by pulling my knitted hat down over my face. Breathing through the weave was annoying at first, but I'd gotten used to it.

By the third day, I'd learned to find grubs quickly in rotten logs near the stream. I'd learned to sneak up on the stream and put the firmly baited hook into the deepest pools if I wanted a fish dinner. My squeamishness at killing a fish by cutting its spinal cord had gone from shaky distaste to a controlled, "Well, I have to do this, so let's get it over with." Cleaning the fish and cooking it on a stick was now easy.

Two days before, when the light had started to go gray and the sky dark, I'd had enough foresight to get everything under cover before a rain storm hit. That day had ended the life of my wristwatch, too. Maybe it was the dampness, but after I wound it, the second hand didn't move and it failed to tick. Tapping it on a rock didn't help, so I'd thrown it away. Now I told time by the sun, as best I could.

The sudden noise of a bird's call or the fire snapping didn't drive my heart up in my throat any more. I still called for Martha, but each day, when no answer came, I'd gotten more used to the idea that she might never come.

While I was sitting and remembering, I had

shifted into a position that cramped my muscles. I was still not accustomed to a world without furniture. I stood and stretched, said, "I'd better get some more wood before it gets too dark." Out of habit, I stopped and listened. Nothing. No engine, no human voice. "What's your choice?" I asked my other self. "Upstream or down?" As it had become harder to find firewood close to camp, I had started to explore further and further away. On the fourth day, I'd gotten lost. Moving uphill, I hadn't paid much attention to direction. After I had collected an armload of branches, I'd turned to head back to camp and realized I wasn't sure which way to go. Everything looked very unfamiliar—the brown and green of this part of the woods differed in tiny details from the part I knew near camp. I'd walked a short distance, then dropped the wood and started to run in panic. By luck, I'd found the stream and was close enough that I could see my white parachute then gleaming through the trees. Since then, I had followed the stream to look for wood, but each time I went out I had to go further for the needed supply.

Remembering that there was a dead tree upstream that still had some small branches left, I headed off in that direction. Besides, I told myself, Betty tended to hang out in that part of the woods, more than downstream. Betty was a tree squirrel that I thought of as my one friend in the forest. She looked like her namesake—a girl at my school who had large eyes and a way of moving quickly. When I'd first seen the squirrel, I'd thought of putting out the animal snares from the survival kit to trap her, but couldn't bring myself to do it. I liked talking to

Betty; she moved and responded to what I said by at least flicking her tail. By now, I was so hungry for company that I would talk to anything that moved.

My own faint trail beside the stream was familiar now, and things like the fallen log bridge across the water or the deep pool where I'd caught the largest trout were known landmarks like a mailbox in front of an apartment or a street sign on a corner. Dave had been right. After you've been in the woods a while, you begin to be able to read it. In the green and brown, green and brown, there are subtle gradations. Thinking of Dave made me think of the other people in my life. If only there was some way I could at least let them know I was all right. Where were they right now? It was late afternoon. Kyle would probably be lying under his Chevy working on the engine, his hands covered with grease ... or maybe he would be meeting Kathy at Zacky's. Would he say, "I wonder if Lisa's okay? A pang ran through me. Quickly I thought of B.J., who would be running her five miles on the sand at Will Rogers State Beach. And Mom—she'd be getting ready to leave her office. Dad was probably in Juneau. . . .

A loud, annoyed chirp broke into my imaginings —Betty! She didn't like intruders. My eyes darted to look through the trees for her, and I saw her high on a branch of a pine tree on the other side of the stream, sitting up staring at me.

"What's the matter? Don't you want company?" I said. At the sound of my voice, she scurried up to the next limb and once again chirped her displeasure. Her tail shivered with each sharp, staccato bark as if my intrusion on her domain was in the poorest of taste. It amused me—the tiny animal daring to challenge the big creature I was. I sat down on a rock beside the stream and watched her. It was nice to have living company, even if that company disapproved of my presence.

"Why don't you come over to my place for dinner tonight?" I called to her. "I'm a gourmet cook with dehydrated food. A regular Craig Claibourne of the campfire." Deciding that my noisiness was just too much for her to remain close to, Betty ran to the end of the branch and without slowing, jumped to a neighboring tree. She wove through the branches as easily as I walked the sidewalks at school until she disappeared from view. It surprised me that there weren't more animals in the forest. The squirrel and a few birds were the only wildlife I'd seen.

I continued on to the dead tree. As I broke off the branches, I was careful to protect my hands from the sharp twigs. "You're turning into a woodsperson, Lisa," I said to myself. Then, "Too bad you're not more into it."

Back at camp, I dumped my load of wood by the fire and as I turned, my glance fell on the pack flap. The seven ink marks leaped out like a message. One week. Since the second day, there had been no sign of a plane. The country was huge, and the small fingers of smoke that I sent up through the trees would be a hundred times harder to spot than any needle in any haystack. This time, I didn't deny the thought. Instead, I walked down to the stream and sat looking at the water, trying to put all the facts together.

When I'd parachuted from the plane, we had not

been just off course, but way off course. The search planes could be miles—hundreds of miles—away from here. I knew that their painstaking crisscross search patterns took a long time. It might take weeks for them to get to this part of the wilderness. And searches were always called off after a certain length of time, with the idea that the people being searched for were bound to be dead. Should I keep waiting, on the off-chance that the planes would come this way? That possibility didn't seem too promising.

How about food? Most of the dehydrated food from the pack was gone. I'd been careful, except for one binge. One day I'd been idly thinking I'd like an ice cream cone, chocolate chip, then had realized how unattainable the cone was. I'd desperately ransacked the survival pack and had eaten two packs of cocoa mix dry. It hadn't helped. I'd still wanted to be sauntering down Santa Monica Boulevard, looking in the windows of the store, casually deciding on a cone, buying it, licking it as I went along the sidewalk, watching the people.

The rest of the food wouldn't last much longer than a few days, in any case. There were fish in the stream, but I had caught only four in seven days. I couldn't live on half a fish a day for too long.

The other choices? There was only one choice—for me to walk out. That's what it came down to—to either stay in this place, hoping to be found, or to get up and go and take the risk. The thought made my heart beat faster. Go? Go where? I didn't have the slightest idea where I was. If I started walking, I could get even more lost. "More lost?" my mind asked. "How could I be any more lost than I am right now?"

Then I remembered the map. Martha's map. When I tried to recall it, parts of it floated into my mind's eye. The mountains had dominated the map, so it had looked like a double-sided fish skeleton, its backbone the ridge of high, snow-capped peaks, and the ribs, the rivers and valleys. Some of the valleys had been white—ice fields. Taking a stick, I tried to draw in the dirt what I remembered of the map—Juneau, Kake, New River. Then I searched my mind for what Martha had said about where we had been. After studying my dirt map and considering the clues, I was sure I was on the western side of the mountain ridge. The terrain, sloping west, backed up my hunch. In the mornings, I'd seen the slant of the sun through the trees, so I knew where east was and that the ocean had to be to the west. I was on the ocean side of that high ridge. When I walked out, it would be generally downhill all the way.

A blue jay flashed overhead and lit in a willow across the creek. With its shiny head cocked, it regarded me for a few minutes before it decided to notify the woods of its interest with a rasping call. When I stood, it flitted off through the branches, voicing alarm. As I walked back to the tent, I kept balancing the pros and cons in my mind. Stay here for how long? Another day? A week? A month? When would winter start? How many weeks before snow and cold would make leaving impossible? How lost is lost?

The sight of my parachute tent in its room in the trees made me realize why I was hesitating. I knew this place. It had become mine. I knew it. A lot of what was holding me back was just that. The stream, the trees, a routine to follow, Betty. Betty

—I'd miss her if I left. For a moment I considered trying to tame her first, so I could take her with me on my shoulder. Reality intervened. Betty wouldn't let me get within a hundred yards of her. She always flicked away at my approach or held her ground and scolded me. Our friendship was definitely one-sided.

The ocean—somewhere to the west. The thought of the blue water—my ocean—waiting there for me tipped the scales. I'd walk out. "Here's what I'll do," I thought out loud. "The stream runs roughly west. Say I walk only a few miles a day. It won't be long before I'm out of the woods, somewhere on the beach. There are towns along the coast up here. The stream has just got to lead to the coast or a river, which could also mean people." My excitement mounted. "There would be a better chance for food, walking, because I can look for berries and better fishing pools. At night I'll set animal snares. And Betty would be too far away to trap, so it would be easier. Any animal I catch will not be a friend."

After the week waiting, the decision to move felt good. Enthusiastically, I started to plan. Much of the afternoon I spent sorting and packing. My clothes presented a problem. I had brought with me a dress and high heels to wear if Dad and I went out to dinner on the night we got back from our trip. The dress already was wrinkled and smelled of wood smoke. I'd have to wash it before I wore it. It lay on the pack, smoothed out as much as I'd been able to smooth it out. Should I take it? It would be useless in the woods. My return plane ticket was just as useless. And there was more. But in the end I decided to take everything. If it all got too heavy,

I could leave things behind as I went.

The parachute had been home to me now for a week. If a real rain storm hit, I'd need a tent. Yet the whole parachute was too big and cumbersome to carry. What about taking part of it? The thought of cutting up the parachute made me pause. Leaving it tied in place on the tree, I stretched it out, then stepped back to get an idea of its size. Trailing on the ground, it seemed huge. There was no way I could take it all with me—I'd have to cut it up. I let my eyes trace imaginary cutting lines on the white cloth, yet I didn't go to get the knife.

The evening moved in with the smell of pine growing sharper—cold, thin, and clean. Suddenly I missed the balmy air of Los Angeles—salt ocean air, and jasmine smelling oriental and heavy in the night. Afraid and homesick, I knew there was no backing down on my decision to walk out. I didn't want to die here alone in the wilderness.

Still, the parachute, spread out like a skirt for a giant, plagued me. I talked to myself. "Look, nobody is going to get upset if it's cut up. It's shelter. I have to have shelter." I got the knife, knowing it was the right thing to do, but even so, I hesitated as I held the blade against the edge of the cloth. It seemed that in some way cutting the parachute would make my decision really final—no turning back. I took a deep breath and sliced through the white cloth.

After that, I decided to wash my hair to get ready for my journey. It had something to do with luck, with going the right way and being found. Down at the stream, I saw myself in a still pool away from the current—my hair was matted and tangled, my face filthy. I filled the pot and heated the water over the fire. Then I wet my hair and with the shampoo from my pack lathered it up. I kept making trips to the stream to get more water to heat to rinse out the shampoo, but it seemed to take forever. Impatient, I finally decided to dip my head in the stream water. Like some Polynesian girl, I thought, kneeling on the bank just before I lowered my head. Romantic. But I gasped as the cold water washed over my scalp. It wasn't romantic at all—just icy cold.

Chapter Six

I zipped up a pocket on the backpack and looked around what had been my camp. I had thought that without the parachute thrown over the branch, the fishing pole leaning against the tree trunk, the backpack lying on the ground, this place would seem like the rest of the woods to me. It didn't. The details were too familiar—the curve of the limb where the parachute had been, the slope of the ground, the bare, burned circle where my fire had been. There were other traces of my presence besides my abandoned hearth: my dirt-covered garbage pit and my faint paths to the stream. It won't take long for the paths to be covered over with grass, pine needles, and leaves, I thought. On one of the trees I'd tied the rest of the parachute by its lines so it looked like a banner. Written across it was the message I'd decided on: AM WALKING DOWNSTREAM, LISA. It had taken a long time to print the words with the ballpoint pen on the slick fabric. The rest of the parachute was to be my lean-to tent, complete with nylon lines to tie it to tree limbs. It was folded now, and tied to the pack with my sleeping bag.

The morning wood supply was ready. I took a stick and dug out some live embers from the fire I'd built the night before, threw on some twigs, and blew them into flames. While I got the morning water, cooked the dehydrated scrambled eggs, and ate one of the three remaining bacon bars, I didn't let myself dwell on my decision to walk out. I ate the eggs slowly, making them last. All I had to do then was clean the pot and pack it, soak the fire with water, stick the knife in its scabbard on my belt. It was time.

The pack felt heavy when I hefted it up and swung it to my shoulders. I'm like a large turtle, I thought, carrying my home with me on my back. Could I carry all that stuff any distance? Should I have taken it all? Yes, I decided. It could be thrown away later if necessary. Lifting the pack so it would ride comfortably, I buckled the hip strap. I could feel my hipbones as I did so—I was thinner.

The fishing pole served as a walking stick. Using it to lean on, I started off. When I got to the stream, I stood for a moment to look back. Would anyone ever see the message on the parachute? With a quick wave, as if to a friend, I sniffed back the tears and moved ahead resolutely.

A few yards down the stream, still in familiar territory, I heard a scolding, chirping sound and looked up to see my little companion, Betty. "You'll miss me when I'm gone," I said to her. "Wait and see." With an impudent flick of her tail, she disappeared behind a tree trunk.

As I had planned, I moved along the water's edge. The scenery stayed much the same at first. Occasionally, I would have to walk around a fallen tree, but the going wasn't too difficult. Once when I stopped to rest, I slipped the pack off and leaned back against a tree. "This is just like my old tree at camp," I said. But I realized that what I had said wasn't exactly true. Back when I'd first landed in these woods, all the trees *did* look alike. But now I recognized the species—spruce, hemlock, cedar, and pine. And if a tree was unusual in shape or size I noticed it. Now the trees didn't seem to be like grim giants judging me an interloper. Now I lost myself among them and was part of the forest. Occasionally, I still resented them for cutting off my view of the sky and keeping the rescuers from seeing me, but mostly I liked being in their midst, where I felt protected. The forest is like the ocean, I thought, as I let the big lodgepole pine take my weight. At first it all seems the same, but then you begin to see that no day is like another, that it changes all the time. The waves have different shapes, some more steep-faced than others. On stormy days, they can turn shapeless and huge—breaking at heights taller than some men—boiling it, throwing foam. But when it's calm, the ocean can look like a lake. And the color of the water changes under the sky—from blue or green to steel-gray. And the waves move at different speeds, at different intervals. The forest is like the ocean. The more you know it, the more you see it and its changes.

The ocean was in my head, but my stomach began to send me signals that I was in the woods and it was time for lunch. I had decided to skip lunch the first day walking to conserve the little food that was left in the survival pack. To forget about eating, I shrugged on the pack and started off again.

The trees were dense now, and the canyon walls on either side of the stream were steeper. Willow and low bushes growing by the stream had become thickets, which I had to walk around. Sometimes the stream seemed to snake along in loops so that I was walking three times the distance I would if I went as the crow flies. But I was afraid to get too far away from the water. My sense of direction was gone. Every morning, I told myself, I would watch where the sun came up to see where east was.

As I pushed and shoved my way through the edges of the underbrush, I began to wonder if walking out had been the right decision. Yes! I said to myself. This way, I might turn a bend in the stream and see a cabin or the track of some logging machine—some sign of people. "Yes!" I said out loud, my voice emphatic, as I slapped another huge mosquito on my cheek. The bugs were thick now, singing around my head, probably because the ground was getting a little marshy. They bred in still water, I knew. Their insistent whine in my ears was all the excuse I needed to stop and rest again, while I took the insect repellent from my pack. I'd stowed it in one of the pockets so I could get at it easily. "If you mosquitoes would just read the label on this bottle, you'd note you're not supposed to like it," I grumbled as I rubbed more of the liquid on my hands and face. They must have heard me, for they backed off to a respectable distance.

B.J. was the one who had trouble with bugs—sand fleas, mosquitoes, anything that bit. When we went to the beach, she'd always come home itching, but she never let it stop her from doing what she wanted to do. As I sat there rubbing on the repellent, I imagined her sitting there with me. Though miserable from bites, she'd just keep going, planning each move. Thinking of her picked up my spirits. Again I shouldered the pack and, using the pole to check the path ahead of me in the heaviest underbrush, I kept heading downstream.

It was about noon when I saw light ahead. I wondered if it might mean an open space, where I could see the sky and some surrounding country, where I could get some idea of what I was walking through. Perhaps there would be a curl of smoke from a campfire. Or signs of a logging camp. As I got closer, I saw sunlight on the bushes. It *was* a clearing!

Standing next to a tall tree, I paused at its edge. The light seemed bright after the dimness of the heavy forest. For a moment, I was dazzled, like a mole coming out of its tunnel. Then I could see clearly. The open space was about the size of a football field. For the first time, I could see into the distance—to where mountains, some with white-capped peaks, stretched in ridges. The closer ones were the color of stone and of pine, but as they receded, they were purple, then lavender, seeming to float like shadows. Ice fields glared, a harsh, blank white. The size of it all made me gasp. Now I could truly sense the scope of the wilderness, and I seemed to shrink in comparison with it. A breeze stirred the tops of the trees, and I could see them form patterns like fields of grain. Half-stunned by it all, I stood there and thought, now I know what grandeur really is.

But nowhere was there a sign of human beings. As my eyes grew more accustomed to the light, I studied the clearing more carefully. The bushes were thick toward the edge, but not down by the stream edge. Something red was growing on the bushes, studding them in clusters. I looked again. Berries! Walking over to a bush, I examined a cluster more carefully. Currants. There were currants on those bushes! The realization made me drop the pack and reach inside it for Dave's book. Quickly I leafed through the pages until I came to the section on fruit. The description of American Red Currant matched the bushes—there was even a picture. And, yes, they were translucent like the description, with a black dot on the bottom.

"Lunchtime!" I shouted, as I pulled a clump of berries from a stem and tried them. Their sweet tartness made my mouth water. They were delicious.

For the next couple of hours I slowly wandered through the clearing, eating as I went and listening to the wind rustle and sigh its way through the trees in the forest. Occasionally, I paused to delight my eyes with the sight of the white-capped vista before me. It was beautiful.

As I ate, I daydreamed. I am sitting with some friends at one of the tables outside the science building at school, and all their attention is on me. Kyle asks admiringly, "Did you really live off the wilderness?" And I reply, "Of course. There wasn't anything else. In fact, I don't think I've ever eaten anything better than the currants in that first clearing I came to...." I turn to Dave, "It was your book, Dave, that convinced me they'd be okay to eat." Kyle glowers, then hitches his chair closer to mine.

The slanting sun told me it was long past noon.

Full and tired, I dreaded slipping back into the heavy pack and pushing on through the dim forest, with its roof of tree branches. It would make me feel closed in, I thought, after being out here in this bright sun. Why not just stay in this clearing for the night? The idea seemed like a good one. It would mean more to eat in the morning. It was windier in the open—that would keep the mosquitoes off. And if I started a signal fire it would be visible to search planes and to anyone who happened to be down there in that seemingly uninhabited wilderness.

In a flat spot at the edge of the clearing I started setting up camp. As I worked, the currants were stirring around in my stomach, and I had a sour taste in my mouth. I made several trips to the stream to drink cold water, but it didn't help. The currants were going to come up. I was frightened. I didn't want to be sick. But it wasn't a matter of choice—quickly I ran into the forest and leaned with one hand against a tree. Holding the trunk for support, I vomited violently. My body shuddered with the spasms. Finally, empty and exhausted, I walked trembling back to camp and sprawled on the sleeping bag. I began to cry. Lost and hungry was enough. Lost, hungry and sick was plain not fair.

It *isn't* fair, I said fiercely to myself. Then the rumbling of my stomach told me it wasn't over yet. I was barely able to stumble a few yards from camp before I started to throw up again. It was worse this time.

What if I had made a mistake in reading the book? What if those berries weren't currants at all, but something else, something poisonous? I turned quickly to the fruit section in the book again. After skimming the pages, I felt relief—the only poisonous berry that grew in this part of Alaska was the baneberry. The berries I had eaten were not baneberries. The currants drooped, the baneberries grew on a straight spike.

I said out loud, "They *weren't* poisonous. Remember the time you ate too many strawberries? The same thing happened then. You just overdid it, that's all. It's just a question of waiting it out."

My voice was shaky. Secretly I knew this wasn't quite like the time with the strawberries. Then, there had been Mother and Dad to give me medicine and sympathy bed to lie in, not this hard ground, and . . . It was happening again. I lurched down to the stream, retching. Dry heaves. Water. I remembered myself at ten with the flu, stomach empty from vomiting, being persuaded by my mother that it was better to drink water even if I threw it up. At the edge of the stream, I cupped water in my hands and sipped it. Then I splashed some water on my face. It felt good. My eyes were puffed from crying, the eyelids red and sore, and my face flushed.

I just sat there, retching again, terrified. I don't want to do this, I thought. It's got to stop right now! My hand shook as I dipped up more water to drink. Then I slumped back, exhausted. It was then that the tough part of me gave the rest of me a lecture: If you quit, you'll die. It was true. This wasn't a game or movie. No one was going to blow a whistle or stop a projector. The forest didn't care one way or the other if this odd creature named Lisa Gallagher lived or died. Deep down below my fear and weakness was a calm center in my mind, where I made my decision. I wouldn't quit. I'd keep moving. "No matter what," I said. "If I have to crawl and pull that pack an inch at a time, I'll do it."

It was getting darker. Using a tree for support, I pulled myself to my feet and moved about collecting wood. My stomach was still a little queasy, but I tried to ignore it. Instead, I concentrated on simple tasks -- lifting a piece of wood, moving the pack, striking matches.

As it grew darker, I used the flashlight to help light my way while looking for wood among the trees. Its beam was now so weak that I turned it on and off as I moved to try and save it as much as possible.

Gazing into the fire later that evening, I sipped the last of the cocoa and thought back over the day. I can't make that kind of mistake again, I thought. In this course, you don't just drop down a letter grade for a mistake or two. No, this one is pass/fail, and one more big mistake could flunk me. And it's not a course I could take over.

Chapter Seven

The morning sun bathed the peaks on the other side of the stream with brilliant light. The air was crisp and still. Lying on my sleeping bag, feeling lazy and drained from being sick, I wondered if I had seen those same mountains from the sky when I was in the M&R plane. The thought brought Martha back to mind. For the thousandth time, I wondered what had really happened to her and why she hadn't parachuted down close to me. The questions didn't really matter. I knew now that there was only a very small chance that I would run into her. Still, after I was up and dressed, I surveyed the landscape for signs of smoke—an early morning campfire that might be hers. But there was only the sea of forest, now still, the mountains, and the ice fields. How far can you see? I asked myself. The distances seemed huge. Would I have to walk to the last range of mountains before I found the ocean? Then I realized that the way downstream was behind me, down through the forest at my back.

Several big blue jays were eating berries from the bushes. I watched them without envy. "I think I'll pass on a currant breakfast," I said. Even today, the acid taste of the currants lingered in my mouth. But gone with the desire for a berry breakfast was yesterday's fear. For a few minutes I thought of moving on, but I knew I was too weak. My vow to "crawl and pull that pack an inch at a time" was not forgotten, but in the bright light of a new day, I decided to make the more sensible decision to rest up and get my strength back, then pick up the pack and walk—I'd get where I was going faster that way.

My mind wandered to a lunch I had eaten with Mother and B.J. During the conversation, Mother had made a comment about the first apartment she had had on her own—it was in the same neighborhood as the restaurant we were in. "I really had a good time there," she had said softly.

"That's what *I* want—my own apartment," I had replied. "I'd like to be on my own."

"And what about when you get sick?" Mother had asked with a quizzical smile on her face. "What then? Who's going to take care of you? Bring you water and juice? Change the sheets?"

Now I knew who it would be from now on—me. I'd certainly taken care of myself the day before, even though I hadn't liked it much.

B.J. had teased me then. "You mean you're not the ideal patient, Lisa?"

"She hardly ever gets sick, but when she does, she makes the most of it," Mother had answered.

"I just like attention," I had said.

Yes, I liked attention, but I could get along without it. I knew that now. And with the realization of my own independence as I stayed alive in the woods was the realization of how dependent I had been before. Mother's and Dad's money paid the rent and bought the food. My teachers filled my head. My friends gave me advice and companionship. But here—there was no one. True, information came to me through a kind of tape recording of Dave's voice in my head. And true, I had to rack my brains to remember things I had learned—from TV, a Sierra Club poster, books I'd read for fun, never thinking that someday I'd be in the same situation as some of the characters I had read about—living off the land.

My stomach, though still sore from the day before, was beginning to ache with hunger. It was probably as empty as it would ever get. I took up my pole and slowly moved down the banks of the stream, which was wider and deeper than it had been further upstream. The loud noise of the water rumbling over the stones had soothed me to sleep in the night. Down near the edge, I dug through the leaves and dirt for worms and soon had several. Then I made my way through the underbrush to where the stream plunged noisily into a large pool. Fitting on the bait, I swung the line over toward the splashing waterfall and let it plop into the water. It floated on the dark, rippling surface for a moment. Then, with a sudden explosion of water, it was gone. I was so startled it took me a second to respond, but the taut pull of the line jerked me into action. I pulled up on the pole as it resisted violently.

A stream of instructions: "Don't lose it. Don't break the line. Don't pull too hard." The trout surfaced to try to throw the hook. As he shattered the water, I pulled the pole back, and he flopped on the bank as the hook came free. Dropping the pole, I dove to get between him and the water. He was a blur of motion as he flipped wildly in the bushes. There! I had him! But his slippery body shot from my grasp. Finally, I got my thumb under his gills and pinned him to the bank. Panting, I brought the other hand up, shoved my fingers under his gills, and lifted him. The fish jerked, but to no avail. He was mine, and he was beautiful. His scales shimmered in the sun; his muscular body must have measured at least eleven inches.

Later, sitting by the fire, smelling the delicious odor of the cooking fish (strange how cooking fish hadn't smelled this good at home), I felt content. I had a daydream of building a cabin of pine logs in the clearing and living there with someone—and the person who came to my mind was Dave! It surprised me at first, but it seemed right that my woods companion should be Dave, and not Kyle. Kyle would do nothing but complain about no television and no roads to race his car on. He would sulk in corners. But Dave—with Dave, I saw myself hunting and fishing, cultivating a vegetable garden. I'd learn to play the guitar and at night we'd sit around singing songs by a fire in a stone fireplace. I felt a smile on my face and longed to tell Dave about the scene in my head. Then I realized that he was more than a thousand miles away and that he didn't even know where I was. Even *I* didn't know where I was. I felt crushed by the silence and the brooding trees on the edge of the clearing.

A movement in those trees interrupted my thoughts. At first I thought it was the wind, but the movement had been only in one place. I saw it again, high up at the edge of the clearing where the bushes thinned out. My heart pounded. Beside the dead tree. Just a glimpse of something black. Bear? *Bear*! Maybe it was a bear who had smelled the cooking fish and was coming to get it. Then the cause of my fear came into plain view—a skunk. A big skunk with a large black-and-white tail carried high over her back, followed by four small skunks with *their* tails held high over their backs, each one a precise distance behind the one before. They looked like tin cutouts moving across a firing range in a penny arcade—they were so alike in the way they looked and moved. With great dignity, they paraded in single file along the other side of the clearing. I relaxed and watched as they made their way busily along. Finally they turned back into the woods.

Staring at the place where they had disappeared, I thought there are animals in these woods, animals that can be caught—though certainly not the skunks! I would put out the snares that night. Animals would come down to the stream to drink. Another fact that I had gleaned from an unlikely place—the La Brea Tarpits, smack in the middle of L.A., at the County Museum, where I had read about a fenced-off black lake, where, millions of years ago, prehistoric animals had come down to drink and died, drowned in the tarpits or killed by predators. Things are still the same in some ways, I thought. A drinking animal, and me, the hunter.

I wondered why I hadn't seen many animals— squirrels anyway—and decided it was probably because I made too much noise when I traveled. While I was walking, they might have been peering at me from the underbrush.

The fish was done. Carefully I placed it on some bunches of green willow leaves that I'd put down on a rock as a makeshift plate. I forced myself to eat slowly to make sure the food would stay down. After eating and cleaning up, I felt better. The shakiness was gone, and I knew I wasn't sick anymore. I toyed with the idea of walking a bit before dark, then decided to stay in the clearing for one more night.

Big, gray clouds full of water were rolling in over some of the distant peaks. Lightning streaked down to the north, and thunder reverberated in the huge stony mountains. It was a display, and I watched it, liking its spectacular drama even as I wondered if I would get rained on again. Then the wind began to push the storm away from me, and the clouds receded into the distance. The thunder was so far away it sounded like faint grumbling.

It was growing dark before I thought again of the snares. I wondered why they had slipped my mind—certainly, here in the clearing I didn't have much to remember. Then the thought occurred to me: what if I do catch something? The thought of my old friend Betty, or her kin, caught in a snare flickered through my mind. "That's it," I said out loud. "The idea of killing something to eat just isn't that appealing." I knew it was true. Yet I'd been able to bring myself to kill the fish I caught. "Fish aren't furry," I said. And the devil's advocate in me answered, "Those steaks you like so much at home don't come from a steer that committed suicide."

What would I do if I caught an animal and it was alive in the snare when I found it? Use a stick on it? I answered myself in an emphatic voice: "If I have to kill it, I'll kill it!" With sudden energy, I took the plastic bag of snares from the pack and emptied it on the ground, which was strewn with pine needles. At first, I was afraid I'd lost one of the snares in the needles, but then I found it—a thin wire with a loop—a noose, really—on one end. The instructions, printed on a single sheet of paper, were simple: find a likely animal trail; position the loop so that the animal, running along, would head into it; tie the other end of the wire to a branch of a bush.

I spent an hour setting up the snares. Down close to the water, with the last snare, I went down on my hands and knees in the soft dirt, trying to decide if what I was looking at was a small animal trail. I was scrutinizing the ground for broken twigs, packed-down earth, and other signs of the passage of squirrel-sized creatures, when I noticed a pattern in the dirt. For nearly a minute I studied it before it dawned on me what it was—a bear track! I felt a shiver of cold fear. I sat down to look at it. It was huge—the paw print of a very large animal.

An old cartoon came back—a hunter is looking at a bear track, and the bear is looking over the hunter's shoulder. I glanced behind me—nothing but tree trunks, light and shade, the red-berried bushes in the clearing. Bears love berries, I thought. In stories about bear-human confrontations, the human is eating berries and looks up to see a huge bear, scooping up berries also, but in its huge paw. I'd only seen a print in the dirt, but adrenalin was coursing through my blood stream. Thoughts moved rapidly through my head. I knew there were bears in this country. They won't bother you unless you bother them (usually), I had read somewhere. They can swim. They are not to be messed with, in spite of their Smokey the Bear image. ... I looked at the print again. Pine needles had fallen into it. That meant it was an old track. Besides, it *looked* old—its edges were crumbling.

Without setting the last snare, I stood, dusted the dirt from my hands, and walked back to camp. As I put some more wood on the fire, I wished for a weapon. All I had was my knife. It would be better to have a gun or a club or a machete or ... a spear! As soon as I thought of it, I felt silly. Sure, and maybe I could do some war dances while I'm at it! Then: what if by some thousand-to-one chance I do have a run-in with a wolf or bear, what do I do? Call a cop? Read a passage to it from a book that says it's not a dangerous animal unless it's provoked? A spear is a good idea. *I'm trained to throw a spear*! Javelin-throwing was a killing art long before it was a sport. Why not? Maybe on the trail I'll see a squirrel or a bird—I might, with practice, be able to kill it for meat. The spear could be used as a walking stick and a fishing pole, too, so it wouldn't be anything extra to carry. It wouldn't *hurt* to have one.

The shadows of the pines lengthened across the clearing and the far-off mountains softened to an almost substanceless lavender in the distance. It was getting on into evening, but there would be time to start the spear before dark. Wood? There was pine, but the branches tended to be curved. I'd need something straighter. Down by the stream was a stand of willows. A willow branch—straight and heavy—would be perfect. I walked down and looked the trees over before selecting one. The first branch I cut off, however, turned out to be too short and slightly bent, so that when I sighted along it, I could see a curve. So I cut another branch, longer and thicker this time, and hefted it in my hand. It felt fine, not as good as the javelin I used at school, but all right. Sweaty from the effort of sawing the limb off, I rested for a moment, then carried it back to camp where I stripped it of twigs and leaves. Then I quickly went to round up more firewood before it got too dark to see. Deciding to forego dinner, I chewed on a piece of beef jerky while I peeled the bark off the spear, smoothed the shaft, and whittled the end to a point.

Then I threw the spear a short distance to see how it handled. It satisfied me—there were still things I could do to it, but it was basically right. I leaned it against the tree trunk at my camp at the edge of the clearing.

Later, as I prepared for bed, I checked the flashlight. Somehow it had gotten turned on by being jostled in the pack. When I pushed the switch up, nothing happened. I unscrewed the end to see if everything was connecting, and everything was. The batteries were dead, and it was useless. Thinking I would throw a branch on the fire to keep it burning whenever I woke up at night, I moved the wood over by my sleeping bag. I could see my spear leaning against the tree. Just before turning in, I went to get the spear and put it beside the sleeping bag, too. Just in case.

Chapter Eight

In the middle of the night I jerked awake, my heart pounding. I lay there, straining to hear through the darkness, unable to see beyond the small circle of light the dying fire cast. Something —a noise?—had awakened me. What? Maybe it was the wind, which was blowing softly in the trees. I felt exposed out in the open. When I had been in the forest, the trees had hidden me, but here I was in plain view under the white parachute tent. What if a bear was attracted to the tent by curiosity?

After a while, as nothing happened, my heartbeat steadied and slowed, and I felt calmer. A half moon was riding over the highest dark peak. Stars, shimmering so that they seemed to move, were thick in the deep sky. The night seemed alive but unearthly, the landscape eerie yet beautiful. I felt awestruck and alone.

When I woke up, it was full light and a different world. I could tell from my raging appetite that I was over all traces of my upset stomach. In fact, my stomach felt like cast iron again, and it wanted food. What was left in the pack? I knew the list by heart—three packs of soup mix, four pieces of beef jerky, and two bacon bars. The people who planned the contents of the survival pack had obviously thought that one week's worth of food would be enough. After that, the survivor was on her own. It had been ten days since I'd parachuted down. I'd conserved the food, supplemented it out with fish, and still it was almost gone.

Maybe there's something in the snares, I thought. After I dressed, I picked up my new spear and moved into the bushes to check. The first snare was hard to find. When I did find it, it was empty. Considering how hesitant I had been to set the snares at first, I was surprised at how disappointed I felt. Locating the other two snares was even more difficult than finding the first. When I had set them, I had been careless about taking note of my surroundings so that I would know exactly where they were. Next time I'll make a clearer mental map, I told myself, then shrugged (hindsight!), stuffed the last snare in my pocket, and went on.

As I approached the edge of the field, a whirring flock of ptarmigan rose and flew into the underbrush. They, like the blue jays, had been after the currants. For a moment, I thought about chasing them into the brush with my spear, but decided that, since they were already alerted, spearing one would be too hard. Instead, I went back to my camp, found a grainy stone, and started to sharpen my knife against it. Dad had taught me years before how to hone a carving knife. The memory of the correct angle for sharpening a blade had never left me. When I was done, I whittled a few more shavings off the spear point. When there was another chance for me to spear game, I'd be ready.

For now, though, I decided, fishing was a better bet. I unrolled the fishing line from the stick on which I kept it in the pack and attached it to my new fishing pole/javelin. In the pack was also a supply of worms wrapped in a used food pouch. I got the pouch out, selected a live worm, and threaded it on the hook. Then I picked out the dead worms, refolded the pouch, and returned it to the pack. I put the pole over my shoulder and went down to the stream, expecting a quick catch.

After an hour, I had only one small fish. Then the hook snagged on a log that had fallen into the stream. When I tried to pull the hook loose, the line snapped. For a second, I considered leaving the hook in the log, but I had only six hooks left. There were no sporting goods stores in these woods, and if I lost all my hooks, I'd be out of luck. The decision was obvious. I took off my boots and waded into the icy water toward the partly submerged log. I could feel stones under my bare feet, and once the rushing water nearly knocked me down. But I got the hook. Back on the dry bank, shivering, I studied the line carefully to see if it was frayed. It looked worn in several spots.

Later, sitting and waiting for the fish to cook, I replaced the frayed line and checked over the rest of my fishing gear. There was still plenty of line. If I didn't try to catch too many logs, the six hooks would see me through. I regretted leaving the two hooks on the stream bottom back at my first camp, but I couldn't do anything about that now.

After I ate, I packed up, ready to move on. By then, the clearing was baking in the sun. It smelled of warm ground and ripe currants. The mountain panorama looked like a Sierra Club poster—with no need for words.

Very gingerly, I sampled a few of the riper currants. Then I shouldered the pack and looked around me with the same feeling that I had when I left my first camp—this was familiar, it was home. The wet remains of the campfire were smoking a little. The air smelled of wet ashes. A circle of freshly overturned dirt marked where I had buried empty food packs and fish bones. I had been especially careful to cover them well. It was not at all logical, I knew, but I had the feeling that if I left any sign of my existence, a bear would lumber up, smell the garbage, associate it with me, and follow me through the woods.

As I started to leave camp, I noticed the now worthless flashlight that I had abandoned at the edge of camp. I started to turn away. Then, deciding the shiny metal cylinder looked harsh and out of place, I buried it, loosening the dirt with my boot heel, then spreading it over the flashlight to make a small mound. I hesitated before leaving. The flashlight had represented a lot—an instant white light against the darkness. I had buried something important. The loss of the flashlight made me feel even more alone.

"If I'm going to cover any ground today, I'd better get at it," I said, my voice low, and started off downstream. As I plunged into the thick growth of trees, I immediately missed the bright openness of the clearing. It was slow going. The brush down by the water was too dense to walk through, and the sides of the canyon were getting steeper. I worked my way through the trees, keeping the stream in sight and following the zigzagging paths I planned with an eye out for the fallen logs, small streams, and stacks of dead branches.

After I had walked for what I thought was more than an hour, I stopped for a break. I lowered the pack from my shoulders and went down to the stream for a drink. When I came back to the pack, thinking I'd shape the spear a little while I rested, I reached for the knife on my belt. It was gone! Panic flooded through me, as I said out loud, "No!" How could I have lost it? Maybe I put it in the pack, I thought. As I started to untie the pack flap to look, I remembered. It was on the log where I had cleaned the fish that morning. I had stuck the knife tip into the wood, telling myself that I'd put the fish over the fire, then come back to wash the knife in the stream. Remembering where the knife was made me weak with relief.

No need to carry everything back with me, I thought. I'll leave the pack here. Yet I didn't want anything to get into my small remaining hoard of food. Ants love bacon bars, I said to myself, and so do raccoons. Lifting the pack, I flipped one of the straps over the stub of a broken limb and pushed my spear against it to hold it in place. Then, looking around carefully to mark the spot in my mind, I started back upstream.

Walking was much faster without the weight and bulk of the pack. Soon the clearing came into view through the trees. I quickened my steps past the old campsite and on to the stream and at once saw the knife sticking in the log where I had left it. As I pulled the knife free, I heaved a sigh of released tension, then went to the stream to wash it clean of dried scales and blood, before putting it securely back in its scabbard.

On the way back through the clearing, I stopped several times to pick and eat only the ripest of the currants. They will keep me from getting scurvy, I joked to myself, a little lightheadedly, happy to have the knife back. Vitamin C, as good as orange juice!

Then, as I pushed through the last group of currant bushes before reaching the woods, a sound—the woof of a dog?—brought me up short. I caught my breath as an animal moved into view. At first I thought it *was* a fat black dog, but only for a second. The rounded ears and the snout told me what it really was—a bear cub, like those I'd seen in the Griffith Park Zoo. A black bear cub. It moved like the baby it was. We had studied each other only for a moment before a roar behind me told me of my mistake.

I started running even as I glanced over my shoulder to see a huge bear—the mother—fangs bared, charging at me through the bushes. Terror gave me strength, and I sprinted into the trees. Thought came raggedly: "You can't outrun her. Dodge when she gets close." She crashed through the brush like a galloping deadly machine. Glancing back, branches slapping my face, I could see her less than twenty yards behind me. She was closing in on me.

Messages sped from brain to feet: jump right, log, run, zigzag. Then my mind turned from words to images. With quick looks over my shoulder, I dodged to keep trees between me and the crashing monster. It was as if there was a place within the terror where my mind and body joined in action without words. My eyes selected the path as my legs moved at top speed, jumping fallen logs, smashing through small bushes. Brush flashed past my eyes, at the edge of vision.

She was even closer. I could hear the panting grunts, imagined hot breath on my neck, claws grabbing me. I didn't see the branch, half-covered with leaves, that lay across my path. I stumbled. Frantically, I fought to recover my balance. My hand reached for a tree trunk too late. As I hit the ground, I tucked my shoulder in and rolled. Pushed by momentum, I was back on my feet and running again. When I looked behind me, I saw her, standing still where I had fallen and following me with her eyes. I didn't slacken my speed.

Finally, winded and shaking, I paused to look back. The bear was gone. I stopped my labored breathing to listen. Nothing. Not a sound of the bear. Weak and panting, I moved down to the stream to drink. My hand was trembling when I dipped it in the water to scoop up a mouthful. Sitting there on the stream bank, I checked to see if the knife was still in its scabbard. It was.

I made my way back through the trees until my pack came into view. I took it down from the tree and struggled into the straps. Tired after the terror of the run, I moved slowly through the forest. The experience with the bear had badly shaken me. I felt frail. How little it would have taken for the bear to rip through skin and muscle to kill or wound me. If it had attacked when my back was turned, or if I had fallen sooner, or if it had continued to pursue me, if any of those things, I might not have survived.

Something like this could happen at any time, I thought. The forest is full of pitfalls—animals, hidden hollows to stumble in. I told myself to stop thinking of such things. I'd face emergencies when they came up, and I'd try to forestall them by careful planning, but to dwell on them was a futile exercise.

So I did what I could about the bear, which was to stop and listen to see if I could hear her every few minutes. The crack of tree branches and popping brush would, I hoped, warn me of pursuit. It was odd—always before there had been something I wanted to hear, like Martha's call or the hum of a plane engine. Now silence was what I hoped for.

For quite a while, I walked, and nothing happened. Then my rubbery legs and the failing light told me it was time to start looking for a spot to spend the night. The trees and underbrush had gotten even denser. The stream was now almost a small river, and I could constantly hear the rush of the water. From the sides of the steep canyon ran occasional small rivulets, tumbling down to join the stream. It was by one of those rivulets that I finally dropped the pack. The forest, seeming heavy with danger, closed in on me.

Telling myself to calm down, I built a small fire. I was hungry, so hungry that I was shaking. My stomach was a hollow, aching void as I untied the pack and got out the pot to fill it with water. "Tonight's menu will be soup, an entree of bacon bar, and perhaps a bit of beef jerky for dessert," I said, not even pretending to talk to another person or Betty.

The aroma of the warming soup made me twitch with anticipation. When it was ready, I stretched out the meal as long as I could, sipping the soup from the pot by using leaves as potholders and taking occasional nibbles of bacon bar. As I ate, I wondered if it was really as delicious as it seemed.

After clearing up, getting more wood, and preparing for bed—tasks I performed numbly—I sat up in the sleeping bag, chewed on the small piece of beef jerky I had saved from dinner, and watched the fire cast dancing shadows through the trees.

"What if . . . ?" I tried to stop the question before it formed in my mind. What if, my mind persisted, I had had the pack on when the bear attacked? I would not have been able to run so fast. What if the bear was tracking me now? I knew this was unlikely, but it stayed in my mind. Nervously, I tried to see beyond the edge of light from the fire, but it was very dark in among the trees and I could discern nothing. My ears strained to hear the slightest noise. I wished for the flashlight, buried back in the clearing.

Then, one internal voice said to the other: You're frightened. You had a bad scare, and it's natural to be frightened. The bear was only a mother defending her young. She's probably holed up in a cave somewhere miles from here. The fire keeps wild animals away, including bears. You're tired, hungry and lost. There's no sense in dwelling on what might happen. You're doing fine. You've been doing okay for nearly two weeks. Hang in there. And the frightened part of me listened without answering.

I slept fitfully. I dreamed of the bear, dressed like Smokey, roaring, arms held up, claws curved to rake, jaws dripping, insane with rage. She reared up and catapulted me awake more than once. I lay there, every nerve tense, every sense straining, tired but afraid to go back to sleep.

The next morning, when I woke up, my hand was stiff from gripping the spear.

Chapter Nine

For the next three days, I walked. Around me, the forest kept changing. Now fallen branches often lay like huge piles of pick-up sticks fallen from a giant's hand, and I was forced to detour around them. The patches of marsh—muskeg, Dave's book called them—were larger and more frequent. But it was the stream that changed the most. When I had first started to follow it, it had been two or three yards across and shallow, so I could see the stones on the bottom under the clear, moving water. Now the stream had become a river, wide as a city street, rushing pellmell within its banks—when it narrowed, the current raged in torrents of white water. I knew why the stream had gotten larger—other streams and rivulets carrying still-melting mountain snow were joining it as it flowed toward the ocean. And *that* meant I was headed in the right direction—away from the mountains which divided Alaska and British Columbia, and toward the coast.

Toward the end of the third day, the rushing

river spread out into a lake. I stood on the shore, slapping mosquitoes, and wondered about lashing some large branches together with nylon line from the parachute to make a raft. I could float downstream then, like Huck Finn. But this wasn't the Mississippi. I thought of how twigs in the white water bobbed, spun, and disappeared, and I was afraid that a raft would turn over and dump my stuff—and me.

A short while later, I continued on my way, and came across a stream, large and swift-moving, that I was afraid to try to wade. I had to backtrack, following the stream up a steep slope, before I could find a shallow place to cross. Then I traveled down, on its other side, to where it joined the river. I decided to camp there that night. It was a good fishing spot, I caught three fairly large trout and ate them all. A feast.

The bear never wholly left my mind. The memory of my run-in with her was like a shadow on the edges of my thinking. Every time I crossed soft ground, I looked for tracks. Several times I saw bear prints, but the only actual animals I had seen were birds and tree squirrels, and then mostly from a distance.

On the fourth night after the bear attack, I sat by my campfire not far from the river and chewed the last piece of beef jerky. I looked again at the marks on the pack flap—fourteen of them. It seemed much longer than two weeks since I had landed in these woods. I was counting time by days-since-deciding-to-walk-out, days-since-the-bear, not in Tuesdays or Wednesdays. I realized I was not aware of what day of the week it was. Memories of home and the people there seemed faded and out of focus. I could not conjure up my parents and friends as I had been able to do in the beginning, and I didn't talk to them much any more, but to myself.

I decided to set my snares earlier in the evening than before, so, postponing fishing until later, I rose from my seat on the ground, and got out the pieces of wire. This time, I worked more carefully than I had before. First, I rubbed my hands hard with pine needles to kill all traces of human odor. Then I went looking for trails. It was easier now to spot them in the underbrush. Droppings and breaks in the walls of scrub were clear signs of the comings and goings of small animals along a path that kept them hidden form larger predators. Without even smiling to myself, as I had in the beginning, I tried to think like a squirrel. A squirrel might notice sticks driven into the ground, so I spent more time finding places close to low limbs and small bushes where I could secure the ends of the wire. Less conspicuous, I decided, pleased with the strategy. Intent, I followed a small trail, seeing where many light feet had indented the ground, finally choosing a place where the brush was quite thick to set the last snare. After marking the locations of the snares on my mental map of the place, I went back to camp to get ready to fish for my dinner.

My stomach was growling with hunger as I baited my hook, attached the line to the pole, and headed on down to the stream. I threw the line into a likely looking dusky-colored pool and waited. Finally, when it was so dark that I was afraid I would snag the line and be unable to find the hook, I gave up. One fish. One very small fish. I looked down at the forked stick with the trout hanging stiffly on it. Then I shrugged. There was nothing I could do about it. One fish was better than none. After cleaning the fish, I drank from the stream, just to put something in my stomach to stop its growling and cramping.

I cooked the fish and ate it down to the last morsel. It did little to abate my hunger. A movement in the trees made me reach for my spear. A squirrel, too high to try to kill. Then the spear in my hand and the fire dancing before my eyes came together in a connection. A black-and-white drawing in a sixth-grade history book in the chapter on "Ancient Man"—men with jutting foreheads sitting by a fire, like this, turning arrows above the flames. The caption described how fire hardened the points. If it had worked for them, it could work for me. I took the spear and turned the point slowly about above the fire, making sure that it did not get hot enough to burn.

The task kept me occupied for a while, then my hunger, which had been there all the time, came to the surface of my consciousness again. I *could* eat a piece of a bacon bar, as a late dessert. I said aloud, "Well, Lisa, for dessert would you rather have a large slice of German chocolate cake with a giant glass of cold milk, or a tiny but delicious piece of bacon bar?" My stomach growled an answer, but I ignored it. "Oh," I continued. "I really think I'd rather just stick to my diet. Just a small piece of bacon bar for me, thank you." I unwrapped a half of a bar and ate it as slowly as I could. Sitting there, dirty, hungry, and lost, I tried to remember if anything had ever tasted better. Now I really know what hunger is, I thought soberly. It has nothing to do with diets. Even when I had fasted for a couple of days in an attempt to lose five pounds before a date with Kyle, I had always known food was available.

In my lightheaded, still hungry state, a vivid image of the refrigerator at home came dancing into my mind. Inside, as it thumped away, were eggs, salami, milk, bread, butter, perhaps some left-over macaroni and cheese, maybe a cold baked potato....

As I drifted into sleep, the refrigerator, now animated and wearing a big taunting grin, frolicked around me. It started to seem almost real, as if it had escaped from my consciousness into the world. Then it faded. Just before the door closed on consciousness, one last thought came into my mind: If I live through this, I'll come out of it a perfect size eight. The thought had an echo: the size eight doesn't matter anywhere near as much as it once did.

A sound! I snapped awake, every sense alert, trying to decipher it. A thrashing in the brush off toward the creek. It stopped for a moment, then started again. It was louder this time. I unzipped my sleeping bag and slowly reached for my spear. The faint light told me it was morning, but earlier than I was used to getting up. I waited, and the sound died away. It had sounded like—what? A fight of some kind? Did squirrels fight for territories? Then it hit me—the snares! Something must have been caught in one of them. For a moment, the idea of a squirrel thrashing and dying in the snare crossed my mind, but I pulled away from the thought. Until the light brightened, I lay there listening and watching. Finally, hunger drove me out of the sleeping bag and into my clothes.

I stirred the ashes of the dead-looking fire with a stick. Uncovering a few live coals that burned red under the ash, I pitched on small twigs and blew the fire into life. As I threw on larger pieces of wood, the flames killed off the morning chill. After making sure the knife was in my belt and picking up my spear, I moved off, in no hurry, to check the snares.

When I approached the third snare, I saw it—a squirrel. A feeling of excitement, of somehow winning, flashed through me. Quickly I walked up to the squirrel, spear ready. What if it wasn't caught? What if it pulled free at the last moment? I leaped forward and pinned the animal to the ground with the spear, but it didn't move. I knelt down and looked more closely. The snare had done its work, the squirrel was dead, the wire noose tight around its neck. I reached down and touched the tail. I remembered how Betty had flicked her tail in indignation at me, how she had leaped gracefully from branch to branch, high in the trees. The fur on the tail was soft and thick. For a second, I wished I had found the snares empty again. I released the wire from the squirrel's neck and picked the animal up. It was limp and slightly warm.

Carrying the squirrel, I went to collect the other two snares. On the way I picked up more firewood. By the time I had arrived back at camp, I had quite a pile. I busied myself taking down the tent and packing my gear. I did not look at the squirrel.

How would I cook it, I wondered. I had the pot, but the squirrel was too big for that, even if I cut it up. I was sure it would be tough if I grilled it as I did fish. Finally I stopped puttering around the camp and faced it: "Okay," I said. "Here's what's going on—you don't want to clean the squirrel. You're doing everything to put it off. But the fact is, you're going to have to do it. You need the food." Besides, what was the point of trapping the animal if I didn't eat it? My stomach had stopped hurting—it was a hollow hole in my body. "All right," I said. "Let's get to it."

I reached down, picked up the squirrel, and carried it over to an old log lying by the stream. I took out my knife.

Why should cleaning a fish be so much easier than cleaning a squirrel? The first cut through the fur was the hardest. The skin, held only by a thin membrane, peeled easily away from the flesh. It was like taking off a glove. I cut off the paws and the head—not easy. Then I slit the squirrel up the belly to the insides. There was a good deal of blood, and my hands were covered with it. I reached inside the squirrel to see how to pull the insides out. I could feel textures—smooth and slippery. My hand came out bloodier.

"Get to it," I said to myself fiercely and put my hand back inside the squirrel to pull out the insides, which were attached only loosely to the carcass. At first they resisted—a slurking sound. Then they fell out on the pine needles. They were better made than a watch: the intestines, wound so neatly; the lungs; the dark red liver and heart. The smell made me want to throw up. Some of the lungs were still clinging to the ribs, and I decided to leave them there. At home I was picky about such things, but here I would eat anything I could, even what the supermarkets called "organ meats." I put the liver and heart back inside the body, after I washed it, then I buried the skin and the rest of the insides in the soft dirt at the stream edge. I washed my hands and walked back to camp.

Putting the meat on a mound of pine needles, I stood looking at it. Decisions. Should I save it for supper at the end of the day's walk, or should I try to cook it now? The thought that it could spoil—and my gnawing hunger—decided me. I'd cook it now and get started walking later than usual.

I quickly cut two green branches, each with a fork on one end. After sharpening the straight ends, I drove the sticks into the ground on one side of the fire, and added a little more wood. "Nothing like a barbecue to brighten up a slow weekend," I said, then I realized after toting up days on my fingers, that it was a Tuesday. I shrugged. I took a long stick and sharpened the end with the knife, then worked it through the length of the squirrel carcass. Brushing away the flies that had been attracted by the odor of the meat, I carried the stick over to the fire.

I pushed some of the blazing wood out from under the forked sticks, then wedged the ends of the long, meat-laden stick in the forks, over the coals. I skewered the liver and heart on a thinner stick, squatted down beside the fire, and held the morsels over the coals. I felt almost happy. The bear had faded as a threatening monster in my mind. I had caught an animal in the snares. I would make it out of the woods, I *knew* it.

In a few minutes, I pulled the stick away from the fire and looked to see if the liver and heart were cooked. It was then that I noticed dark, dried blood under my fingernails and in the cracks of my knuckles. I am a killer, I thought briefly, without much emotion, but the thought left my mind when I saw that the heart and liver were done. After blowing on them to cool them, I ate them quickly. "Hors-d'oeuvres," I said. "Tasty." And I licked my fingers.

The other meat was nowhere near done. "Two choices," I said. "More fire or drop it lower." I knew I could not afford to spend too much time cooking, and I hated to build up the fire. If I did, the flames would blacken the meat and burn the outside before the inside was done. I took the end of the stick the meat was on and lowered it to the ground. Although the stick was now at an angle, with one end in the fork and the other on the ground, the meat was closer to the fire. I felt the end of the stick to see if it was going to get so hot it would burn. No, it was hot, but not too hot, and I could watch it.

After a while, the meat began to darken on the bottom. I kept adding sticks to the fire, and as they burned down, I pushed the embers under the meat. By using a rock to hold down the end of the stick, I could turn the meat and cook the spots that seemed raw. As I moved about, I would sometimes catch a whiff of the cooking squirrel and my mouth would water.

At last I couldn't wait any more. I moved the rock and checked the end of the stick to see how hot it was. It was cool enough to handle, so I picked it up and lifted the meat from the fire. Careful not to drop it in the dirt, I managed to cut off a bite-sized piece. After juggling it with my fingers and blowing on it to cool it, I popped it into my mouth. The flavor of the juice was heavenly. I started to chew it, but it was like tasty rubber—the toughest meat I had ever tried to eat. I kept chewing.

The joint where my jaws met began to ache from chewing, so I finally decided to save the rest of the meat for the night. Perhaps if I simmered it with something berries—I'd check the book—it would become a little more tender. I thought this, but didn't believe it.

Chapter Ten

With the squirrel wrapped in the foil from a soup pack, the fire soaked, I put on the pack and picked up the spear. "Let us then be up and going, with a heart for any fate . . ." As soon as the words came from my mouth, I burst into laughter. Now where did *that* come from? I instantly knew—Mrs. Zimmerman, sixth grade. I could see her, a distant picture from the past—frizzy brown hair, loafers, dark skirts and white blouses always the same, and that smile that broke out on her face like a sunrise at a sign of scholarship from one of us, a new idea, or something beautiful.

She was always in disarray, always excited and fierce about ideas, as if she were plugged into a socket. She was still my favorite teacher, though I hadn't thought of her in months. She took us blasé L.A. brats and turned us on to the whole wide world. She'd come charging into class as she went charging everywhere, excited about a bug or a poem or an equation.

As I started walking, I said, "When I get back,

I'll go to visit her and tell her how I quoted her verses in the middle of nowhere." Except to her this place would not be nowhere, but *somewhere*. Picking my way through crazily fallen branches, I tried to remember the rest of the poem. Longfellow —corny old Longfellow. "Life is real! Life is earnest?" Yes, that was part of it, and the title . . . the title was "The Psalm of Life." "Tell me not in mournful numbers, life is but an empty dream . . ." I recited as I pushed my way through a thicket. And "lives of great men all remind us, we can make our lives sublime," as I trudged along. For almost an hour, walking, I dredged my mind for the rest of that poem and put it slowly together. Meanwhile, my legs almost automatically were taking me along the rough path laid out ahead of me by another part of my mind.

And then I noticed that the foliage down by the water was different. "Psalm of Life" receded into the background as I worked my way closer through the brush to have a look. Bushes taller than I bordered the river. As I got closer, I saw purple berries in clusters on the branches. I shrugged off the pack and reached for the book. Serviceberries, edible, can be used to make muffins or can be eaten raw, the print said. The berries and leaves on the bush matched the picture and description on the page. I ate only a few, though they were delicious, then got out the pot and filled it with them. Taking one of my shirts out of the pack, I wrapped the pot in it so the berries wouldn't spill and put the whole thing in the top section of my pack. Maybe they would tenderize the rest of the squirrel for dinner that night.

After that, I ate some more berries, reveling in

the sweet juice as it went down my throat. When I reached the next small stream, I stopped to drink. My stomach had accepted the berries, and I knew I wouldn't be sick this time.

Later in the afternoon, I heard a sound that I thought at first might be thunder. Yet it didn't stop, as thunder would, but steadily rumbled on. It made me uneasy. As I moved downriver toward the noise, it increased until it was a roar. A waterfall! Of course! A waterfall goes over a cliff or drop of some kind, I thought, so I moved carefully, trying to see ahead through the trees.

The trees fell away, and the ground shook from the force of the plummeting water. I moved up, thinking, what if I can't get down? Then it was there before me—the river throwing itself with white fury through the narrow rock gap, falling in a long, heart-stopping plume of water to the stream bed below.

I leaned back against a tree to take some of the weight of the pack off my shoulders and studied the situation. It was not so bad. If I stayed back away from the river, the canyon wall was steep, but there were plenty of trees to help me climb down. Only in the middle of the canyon where the water had worn the land to bedrock was there a sheer drop of about thirty feet.

I used my spear to check my footing, and tapping it along in front of me to gauge the danger of fallen log jams and cracks in the rock, I made my way from the top to the bottom of the cliff along the edge of the canyon. Once when I stopped to rest, I looked back at the river flinging itself down the rock wall. Mist rose in clouds. It felt cool against my perspiring cheeks.

When the waterfall was behind me, the ground leveled out a bit. The exertion of climbing down had made me thirsty, and I looked ahead anxiously for a small stream where I could get a drink. When I glimpsed water through the trees a short way ahead, I quickened my stride, though my legs were weak from the climb. Carelessly, I stepped on, rather than over a small log, and as I did, I could feel the bark break away under my foot. I began to fall. To save myself, I jerked my foot forward. It hit the ground at an angle, with most of my weight on it. A hot, sharp flash of pain made me cry out. Luckily, my spear took part of my weight. I was able to push sideways so that I didn't sprawl face first. When I hit the ground, it knocked the wind out of me. I lay there for a minute, gritting my teeth against the pain and trying to get the air back into my lungs. All the while, I talked to my ankle: please, don't be broken—hurt if you have to, throb like crazy, but don't be broken.

As my breath came back, I wiggled free of the pack, sat up, and started to pull the foot up where I could see the ankle. The movement made the pain worse, so I rested the leg out straight and lay against the pack. Closing my eyes, I waited for the pain to subside.

"Lisa, old girl," I said in a scolding voice, "You've made another one of those mistakes—the kind you might not live through." I answered myself, "Oh, come now, let's not overdramatize." I remembered spraining my ankle playing volleyball at the beach the summer before; it had hurt more than this, and I had lived through the experience. And my sarcastic side said silently, sure, so we'll just zip down to the doctor as we did then and pop by the drugstore for an ace bandage and slap on some ice packs for the pain.

I opened my eyes to look down at the ankle. The pain had settled into a dull throb. I reached down and pulled the leg up gingerly, careful not to hit it on anything. Resting the calf of my leg on the other thigh, I carefully unlaced the boot all the way and eased it off. Then I peeled down the sock. My ankle was swollen, the skin shiny with tightness, but the swelling was not so bad as it had been when I sprained it before. The ankle bone was barely visible under the puffiness.

I thought, if ice packs help, how about ice water? The stream was only a few feet away. I tied the boot to my pack, stuffed the sock inside, then with the help of the spear and a tree, I pulled myself upright. When I tried to put weight on the bad ankle, it gave under me as a shot of pain zipped through it, and I almost lost my balance. Quickly I sat back down. In a sitting position, I scooted forward, holding my injured foot out of harm's way. Then I reached behind me to pull my pack and spear up. And so I inched my way along, scooting forward a few feet, then bringing up the pack and spear, until I reached the bank of the stream. Once I bumped the bad foot against a log, and the flash of pain made my eyes water.

Sitting on the bank, I eased my foot into the icy water. I took stock of my surroundings, then said to myself, "Not my first choice for a camp site, but it will have to do, I guess." Mosquitoes settled into a cloud around my head, and I reached into the pocket of my pack for the insect repellent.

After a while, I lifted my foot out of the water to take a look at the ankle. It was still slightly plump, but the swelling had gone down a little. I could wiggle the toes and even move it up and down. I knew it wasn't broken.

I spent the hours of remaining daylight collecting small branches within arm's reach for firewood, arranging the sleeping bag, and doing what I could to set up camp. I built a fire, then got out the shirt-wrapped pot and foil package of squirrel. I used the shirt to dry my foot, then slid the foot partway into the sleeping bag to keep it warm. Awkwardly I cut the meat from the squirrel bones, added it to the serviceberries in the pot, then scooped a little water from the stream with my hand and dumped it into the pot, too. A squirrel stew.

Gnawing on the squirrel bones as I waited for the stew to cook, I thought of how I would have looked to the folks back home. Lisa Gallagher, who always noticed a dirty fingernail or speck on a skirt and did something about it, was sitting by a smoky fire in smoke-smelling, reeking, filthy clothes, no bath for weeks, hair matted, covered with scratches and scabs from tree branches and falls, gnawing like a savage on half-done squirrel bones. In spite of my aching ankle, I had to laugh.

I tested the ankle again. It hurt, but not seriously. There was nothing to do but wait and see how stiff it was in the morning. Anyhow, it wasn't broken, which was the important thing.

After an hour had gone by, I decided the stew was done, and took it off the fire. As I waited for it to cool, I broke up wood for the fire. Though the squirrel meat was still tough, the stew was quite good, better than I had thought it would be. The sweet, acid taste of the berries went with the squirrel the way cranberry sauce does with turkey.

The light was fading. The day had been overcast, and I sensed that it was getting dark earlier than usual. That could mean rain during the night. The tent was still tied to the pack, and I was using the poncho as ground cover under me. A good heavy rain could soak the sleeping bag·so that it would take days to dry. It wasn't worth the chance. Tossing more wood on the fire for light, I put a boot on my good foot and a sock on the injured one. Hobbling, I untied the tent from the pack and put it up, then moved everything under it, including what was left of the wood.

My ankle was throbbing from moving around. I spoke to Mrs. Zimmerman: "How about an epic poem for me, one about a brave, one-legged woman lost in the woods? And how about having it end with a piece of hot apple pie and a warm bed?" But Mrs. Zimmerman came back instead with something about a "youth who bore mid snow and ice, a banner with the strange device—Excelsior!"

I didn't sleep well, but woke often to change my position in the hopes of finding a comfortable spot for my ankle. And all night I had a recurring dream in which a large, vicious bear dragged me through the forest by my foot.

Chapter Eleven

Rain was misting down when I woke up the next morning. It's a good thing I put up the tent, I thought, as, still in the sleeping bag, I tested out the bad ankle by flexing it and moving it from side to side—though stiff and sore, it was better.

Staying under the tent to keep dry, I got dressed. It was awkward because I couldn't stand up, but I managed to put on my left boot, then decided to try a boot on my swollen right foot, too. Limping would be more efficient than scooting in a sitting position. To avoid unnecessary pain, I kept on the sock I had worn all night. After loosening the laces of the boot as much as possible, I began working the boot on the foot. It hurt a little, but I could tell by the way it felt that I was not injuring the foot more by moving it, so I kept struggling until the heel of my foot finally slid down inside the boot, then laced it up loosely. With the poncho draped over my head, I scooted out from under the tent and reached for the low branches above me to pull myself up. Rain water from clusters of needles poured down on the poncho.

When I put weight on the foot, keeping the pressure mostly on the toe, I found I could limp. After a few experimental steps, I leaned against a tree, all my weight on my good leg, to plan the day. I toted up my food inventory in my head: squirrel bones, two soup packs, and half a bacon bar. A mixture of bones and soup mix was tempting, but it required a fire, which would be difficult to start in the rain. I wanted to save the bacon bar. Finally, I said, "Today, folks, is high-protein, rest-and-half-rations day in the Gallagher Diet Plan." It would be a good day for fishing, I thought, since I couldn't walk any distance at all. And by the time I'd caught something, perhaps the rain would have stopped.

Settling for a breakfast of cold water, I rolled the sleeping bag and put it and the pack back under the tent. The poncho would be clumsy to fish in, so I put on my down jacket, which was waterproofed. Everything was in slow motion; every step and movement I made was studied. I did *not* want to turn that ankle again. The thought of twisting it put my teeth on edge.

Sticking the leg out in front of me like a Russian dancer, I lowered myself to the ground next to a rotten log and picked through the bark for grubs. After I had captured several, I folded them in the foil wrapper with the leftover worms, now half-dead, took my spear and fishing gear, and worked my way down to the river. The spear had become a cane.

The river was now full-flowing, wide as a boulevard, deep enough so that the water moved slowly. I baited the hook with a grub, and, shifting into a position that favored my bad leg, I swung the baited hook out and let it drop into the smoky blue water.

Even with the light drizzle and aching ankle, I was almost content sitting there. I remembered Dad's description of this country and knew what he meant. The land *did* give a quiet, peaceful feeling of solitude. (Leaving out the bears, I added.) I thought that if he were here with me and we had plenty of food and could leave when we wanted to, I would enjoy the experience. The backpacking trip, I knew now, would have been much more fun than I had anticipated.

A daydream ran itself through in my head: Kyle and I setting up camp, his surprise at how well I do things—putting up the tent, gathering wood, starting the fire. But then reality shouldered its way into my reverie, and I could see how it would really happen. Kyle's face, as he stared at me with a cold expression of boredom, flashed into my mind and stayed there, until I turned him around and brought him back as Dave, smiling and excited about being in the wilderness.

I pulled the line slowly through the water, then let my thoughts wander again. I was beginning to think of Kyle as coldly as he had often thought of me. What had I liked about him? The look in his eyes? His long-nosed profile? The way he laughed (sarcastically)? His aloofness? It didn't matter. And Dave? Whatever might happen with Dave didn't matter either—not here, not now.

My thinking was changing. Alone, I was remembering a whole panorama of my childhood and early adolescence. Mrs. Zimmerman and sixth grade. Old songs from when I was seven. A picture in a school book. A visit from an aunt who lived in

Oklahoma when I was five—she'd worn a fur coat that I'd liked to stroke. . . . A pull on the spear jerked me back to the present. Quickly I tightened the tension on the line and it snapped out of the water. I had missed, but the fish hadn't. He had stolen the bait and left me with an empty hook.

"Well, now, let's be fair," I said to the fish, who was swimming free somewhere below the surface. "You got your breakfast. Now I want mine." I baited the hook with a worm and dropped it back into what I thought was the same spot. The fish must have felt the hook graze his jaw the first time and was running scared, because nothing happened. It was getting suspicious of food that fell from the sky. Manna with a hook attached.

The ankle began to throb softly, and I considered taking the boot off and putting the foot in the water. Then I decided to wait until I got back to camp. Walking any distance seemed a near-to-impossible activity. Watching the water flow past, so easy, on its way to the ocean, I thought again of rafting down the river, letting the current take me. If my ankle stayed tender, it might be a good idea, I thought. Then I remembered once more the rushing stretches of white water in the river when it narrowed and the roaring waterfall. It was too risky.

This time when the pull came on the spear, the line didn't go slack as I pulled back. I flipped a shimmering trout far back on the bank and soon had killed him and impaled him on a branch. By what I guessed to be almost noon, I had four fish on that branch. I had hoped for more. For once, I wanted to be completely full, and I wasn't sure that four trout, even with squirrel-bone soup as an appetizer, would do it. I cleaned the fish, leaving their heads on so I could string them on the stick to carry them.

By the time I got back to camp, rounded up dry firewood, and started the fish and soup cooking, my foot was aching again. I sat down by the stream, took off the boot and sock, and slid my foot into the cold water. It took only a few minutes for the pain to subside. I wasn't doing badly as my own doctor.

The drizzle had stopped, and splashes of brilliant sunlight sparkled on the surface of the river. Then I saw a large bird soaring high above the water—high, far higher than the blue jays seemed to go. He swooped down on an air current, riding it, and I saw him clearly—an eagle! His white head and dark plumage marked him well. He must have seen something—a mouse or a squirrel—on the ground, for his circles became tighter. Then he plummeted toward earth.

It sent a thrill through me to see the eagle wild and free. I ached to share it with someone. Mother, B.J. . . . Dave, of course, and Mrs. Zimmerman! I could see her standing, hair in happy disarray, arms outstretched, saying, "Look! Just look at that, will you!" And she would quote Tennyson in a triumphant voice, dramatic—just enough to keep us sixth-graders on that edge of embarrassed laughter/emotional insight: "And like a *thunderbolt* he falls!"

Funny, those poems that had seemed so old-fashioned, close to ludicrous, in a sixth-grade classroom overlooking a parking lot, a recording studio, and Santa Monica Boulevard, seemed to fit the wilderness more than anything I had read since.

Mrs. Zimmerman knew. She knew what made life worth living. She, years before the macho men in the beer commercials, had gone for the gusto.

The aroma of the cooking fish pulled me back to now, and I dried my foot with my handkerchief, worked the sock and boot back on, and moved to the campfire. The soup first. I drank it, noticing that the bones had added something to the somewhat artificial taste of the freeze-dried soup—calcium? I cracked the bones and sucked out the marrow. By then, the smallest fish looked done, so I took it off its stick and slid it onto an old food pouch. Before I ate the fish, I picked up pieces of it with my fingers and blew on them to cool them. I finished eating the small fish just as the next was ready. In fifteen minutes, I was through, every scrap of fish gone and nothing left but the bones and heads. Yet as I licked the oily traces of fish from the food pouch, I realized I was still hungry and wondered if I would ever be full again.

Using the sleeping bag as a pillow, I spread out on the poncho to relax and doze. The terrible urgency that had seemed to push me along at first now seemed to have eased up. Even with an injured leg and not much food, my confidence was high. It had grown day by day. Through the haze of sleep a thought formed in my mind: I have made it alone. No place to go for help, no one else to ask or blame, no institutions to make things easy—nothing. And I had made it through. No one I knew had ever done that—not Mom, not Dad, no relative, no friend. All their lives, they had had someone—a relative, a friend, a doctor, a policeman, a stranger. But I had done it without anyone, alone. In the wilderness, lost, injured, and underfed, I felt more alive than I ever had in my whole life. Smiling to myself, I closed my eyes.

I must have slept for several hours, because when I woke up, the light was softer, and the sky again was overcast, heavy with coming rain. Although my ankle was stiff, I laced up the boot and went to gather firewood. As I collected the wood from under the thick branches of trees, where it was drier, I kept an eye open for spots to put the snares. Down by the river was a place that looked promising. After dumping the last load of wood under the tent, I took out the snares and spent the last of the daylight hobbling around setting them up by the water. I had read in the book that willow tips and leaves were good sources of vitamin C— the Eskimos dipped them in seal oil and ate them, particularly in spring. I tried chewing on some of the tips which seemed youngest. They were tasteless. The leaves had a weird texture, like felt, but I ate them anyway. I snapped off some twigs to take back to camp.

Under the tent on the sleeping bag, I nibbled on the green twigs and told myself that tomorrow it was back on the trail, ready or not. Even with an occasional twinge from the ankle, I slept well.

When I woke in the morning, I worked the ankle up and down. It was still sore, but much better. The skin was purple but the swelling was gone. It would be all right to walk, I said to myself, as long as I took my time.

Then I went to visit the snares. Ever since I had trapped the squirrel, I looked forward to checking the snares as if it were Christmas morning. I dressed and made the rounds. Nothing. After I collected the snares, I started to open the pack to put them away, then stopped.

"Lisa, I think today is lighten-the-pack day," I said, thinking of the burden of the heavy load on my back and the effect it could have on my tender ankle. I sat under the tent and pulled everything from the pack and emergency kit onto the poncho. I looked it all over. No question that I would take with me the fishing equipment, pot, matches, first aid kit, and nylon lines from the parachute. My soap was only a sliver now, very light, so I decided to keep it. The shampoo bottle, though, was full and heavy. My hair could go without washing. I put the shampoo bottle in the discard pile, along with my toothbrush and tube of toothpaste. I could use twigs to clean my teeth, then throw them away, as the Indians did, and besides that, I wasn't getting the chance to eat anything sweet that would cause cavities. To the discard pile I added my hairbrush, all my makeup, my dress, my high heels, and an extra pair of shoes. Because it weighed little, I would take along my money; the green bills looked worthless (and were worthless) here in the forest, like play money. The plane ticket was light enough to carry, too. Matches, of course—twenty-two were left. Six fishing hooks. The sleeping bag and poncho. Soup mix and piece of bacon bar. All "take with."

Looking down at the pile of discards, I felt a pang of sadness as the bright yellow and blue of the print dress caught my eye. But it was no use to me at all here.

I quickly took down the tent and packed all the things that were going with me. I hefted the backpack to check its weight—it was considerably lighter. Then I stowed all I was to leave behind in the small survival pack and hung the pack by one of its straps to a tree limb. I wondered if some time someone would find it there and try to figure out why anyone had taken a party dress and high heels out into the wilds. Using the pen, which was writing paler and paler, I wrote a note on the envelope that had held the plane ticket: WALKING ALONG THE RIVER SOUTHWEST, LISA GALLAGHER. Then I put the note in the survival kit so it would be protected a little from the rain, and stuffed the plane ticket itself deep in the backpack, on the bottom.

It was time to go. Picking up the backpack again, I shrugged into it and buckled up the waist strap. Spear in hand, I started out. Planning every step, I moved slowly through the woods. My left leg got tired from the extra effort of favoring the injured right ankle, so I rested often.

Now there were more wet and marshy places covered with willow and low bushes. I stopped to rest beside one of them that was big enough to form a small clearing. I pulled some of the willow tips toward me and broke off the tops to chew. As I did, I noticed some ferns at the edge of the wet ground. I sat down beside them and pulled out the book. Too bad it wasn't spring, when the young curled fronds poked up; they tasted like asparagus, the book said. But the outer leaf stalks were edible, too, and could be roasted. I dug down into the dirt and found some—they looked like tiny bananas. I put them in the pack. That night, I decided, I would make a study of the book to find out about plants and roots I could eat.

As I dug out more leaf stalks, I gazed around to see if anything else looked edible and noticed a few red berries in the wetter part of the clearing. At first I dismissed them as holly berries, which I knew weren't edible, then I looked again. They weren't holly berries! They grew on a bush that did not have holly leaves. Holly leaves are bright green and spiky and these leaves were nothing like that. I went back to the book. I had just about given up trying to find out what the berries were, when a picture caught my eye. "Low-bush cranberry," the caption said. I put the book, now dirty and dog-eared, back in my pocket. Then taking my spear (still partly serving me as a cane), I picked a path through the marshy ground by stepping from bog to bog until I reached the nearest cranberry bush. I bent down and pulled off one of the red berries. It looked like a cranberry—Thanksgiving, home-made cranberry sauce, the bad ones float. I bit into it; it was so spongy and so tart, it puckered my mouth. No doubt. It was a cranberry. The sharp taste reminded me a little of the currants, so I ate only a few raw, then picked some to add to the fern leaves and willow shoots.

Back at my pack, I put the hoard of food into the pot and once again wrapped it with the shirt to keep it from spilling.

The rest of the day was spent making slow and careful progress. I could feel my legs swinging, from the hip, carried like pendulums with the momentum of the last step, coming down harder on the left to favor the right. I was walking like a zombie most of the time, awakened only by twinges of pain that came with every small misstep, and a bend in the river around which I hoped might be something—a house, a person, a boat. . . . Once in a while, I counted my steps, telling myself to go only a hundred more before stopping. Then I would rest and go on, because maybe around the next corner would be . . .

As the day wore on, the ankle seemed to improve, and by the time night came, I figured I had covered at least two miles, maybe a little more. For dinner, I ate the last soup pack, saving the fern hearts for the next day. I was too tired to bother with them.

Chapter Twelve

By mid-afternoon of the next day I was too tired and ravenous to go on walking. My legs were trembling, and though my ankle was better, I didn't want to take a chance on turning it again. So I set up camp on a stream bank, then went down to the river to fish. As I dug for fresh bait, using a stick in the loose dirt by the edge of the stream, I saw my hands shake with fatigue and hunger. Still, I forced myself to work slowly and carefully as I tied the line to the spear and moved silently up to a deep pool that had formed where the stream poured into the river. The surface of the water was dark and rippling. I fitted on a large grub and swung the line out over the water to drop the bait. It never reached the river. While it was still almost a foot above the surface, the water exploded as a fish lunged in an arc to grab the bait. As I jerked back in surprise, the fish—a trout—flipped into the current to run for it. The pole arched. I frantically tightened my grip and pulled. The fish came out of the river in a shower of water and thudded heavily on the bank as the hook came free from his mouth. He was too far away to grab, and I didn't trust my bad ankle enough to jump to him. Almost without thinking, I quickly jabbed the sharp tip of the spear through the fish's body and impaled him to the bank.

The spear shaft vibrated with his efforts to twist free as he writhed and flapped on the ground. Excitedly, hand over hand, working my way down the spear shaft, I knelt to him, pulled my knife from my belt, and sawed his spine with the blade until the bone snapped and he died. The trout was almost twice the size of any fish I had caught. Encouraged, I kept fishing, but to no avail. Finally, hunger drove me to cook dinner—fern "bananas" and berries in the pot with some water, and the fish, which I grilled over the flames.

With the pot boiling and the fish sizzling on the fire, I sat cross-legged on the poncho, chewing some willow twigs, for a while. Then I got up to make a plate by stripping leaves from a willow branch and spreading them out on a rock. The bare wood of the branch gave me an idea—I'd carve a spoon to eat my stew with. So far I had been sipping from the pot—more than once I had burned my mouth—or using the knife as an eating utensil, risking getting cut. I took the knife and whittled first one side and then the other of the willow branch, watching the green bark separate from the white inner wood. Then I hollowed out the middle of one side.

By now the pieces of fish (I had split it in two) looked almost done, so I took everything off the fire and sat down to eat. The spoon worked better than I thought. I'll make a fork, too, I told myself, thinking how easy it would be to carve a two-tined fork from a branch at the place where it made a Y. As for the stew, it tasted fine. It could have used a little salt, perhaps, but otherwise it was good. By the time I had finished it and the fish down to the last bit, I was already planning how I would keep a sharper eye out for berries, greens, and roots from then on.

Some camping trip, I thought—it's a camping trip in every sense except that it's for real, live-or-die, total survival. If I weren't lost, it would be recreation. My stomach, not full but momentarily satisfied, was quiet for a while, and I was content.

I watched the shadows of the tree branches flicker in a slight wind on the surface of the stream, and I thought that human beings would be healthier if they lived like this—roughing it, living off the land—and maybe even happier, if they were given a companion. I had to laugh at myself. If I was so much in love with the woods, how come I was trying so hard to get out of it, looking around each bend in the river for a sign of people? I would have been ecstatic to see a discarded Coke can on the river bank.

After straightening up camp, I went to the stream to soak my ankle. It was better. Most of the swelling was down, and I could move it with only a little soreness. I dried my foot with a shirt and put my boot back on, then got out the snares and set them. When I got back to camp, I was yawning, though it was still light. Walking and favoring my bad leg had been even more work than the long day of tramping I had become accustomed to. "So tomorrow I jog all day to make up for lost time," I said sleepily after putting on insect repellent (almost gone) and pulling the wool hat down over my face.

As soon as I woke in the morning, I experimented with the ankle. Though it was a little stiff from the night's rest, I could move the foot in a circle with only a little discomfort. Satisfied that I'd be able to walk, I turned my mind to thoughts of food.

"Perhaps a piece of bacon bar wouldn't hurt," I said. This time the thought that the bacon bar was the last of the survival pack food didn't alarm me. I got everything ready to go before taking the half bacon bar out of the pack, unwrapping it, and breaking it in two. For a moment I paused, salivating, then rewrapped the larger of the two pieces and put it back. Maybe I'd just keep breaking what was left of the bacon bar in two, eating one piece, and keeping the rest for the next day until I was down to a crumb. That way it would last for days. I went to sit by the stream, where I took sips of water and tiny pieces of bacon bar, sipping and eating, wondering, How much farther? Maybe downstream only half a mile away was a road or fishing lodge or lumber camp. When I had first started walking, I had thought of course of getting out of the woods and back home. But it had seemed unreal. Now the thought had to do with here and now; I had walked far enough to believe in the reality of getting out. I could envision how the trip would end—I would find a circle of ashes where a campfire had been, a trail, or people. In fact, it all became *so* real that I hurriedly finished off the piece of bacon bar in my enthusiasm to get moving.

When I stood up, though, my jeans bottoms fell down over my shoes. I had lost so much weight, the jeans were drooping around my hips. As I walked, I kept tripping over the legs of the pants, which were trailing on the ground, so I cut a length of parachute line to make a belt. When I tied the line and hitched up the waist of the jeans, I saw my hip bones sticking out sharply. My belly was hollow with hunger.

Around a bend of the river, after about two hours of walking, I came upon a marshy open space almost as big as the first clearing I'd found. My first thought was "bear." So I stood back under the trees in shadow and carefully searched the clearing with my eyes for signs of wildlife. There was something—not a bear, but another covey of ptarmigan feeding under the bushes, scratching and making soft noises. They were like hens, so much, I thought, that if I didn't know better I'd think I could lure them by calling, "Here, chick, chick, chick." If I could just get closer. . . . Fading back into the forest a few paces so they couldn't see or hear me, I eased the pack off and lowered it slowly against a tree. I noted details in the surroundings—a dead branch, a gap in the underbrush, a large tree that stood alone—so I would be able to find the spot where the pack was. Then I stole back into the clearing.

The birds were closer to me now. The light wind rustling the bushes helped hide the noise I made as I stealthily crept toward them. I hadn't gotten very far into the clearing before one of the birds cocked its head suspiciously in my direction, listened, then spotting me, sounded the alarm. As the birds scattered in a flurry of feathers and squawks, I took quick aim and let fly with the javelin. I almost got a ptarmigan. It dodged at the last moment, just barely evading the spear. I ran, limping, to get the spear to try for another shot, but by the time I got to it, they had disappeared into the woods. The clearing was empty. The disappointment of missing the bird was countered by optimism—the throw had come very close. Another half inch and I would have hit the bird.

Wiping the wet dirt from the tip of the javelin on a bush, I decided that when I got back to school, I would encourage the coach to include a competition for accuracy as well as distance in the javelin event. I smiled at the thought—it showed I was counting on surviving this ordeal to be in school in the fall.

I went back to get the pack and brought it into the open space, took out the pot and started searching for berries. There weren't as many as before, and after an hour I had filled only half a pot for my trouble. Then I noticed that the wind was blowing and the overcast sky had darkened. It was time to be moving on. Shrugging into the pack, I moved across the clearing and back into the forest. It wasn't as blustery in among the trees, but I could hear the wind moaning in the tree tops.

A little later, when the first rain drops splattered down through the branches, I untied the poncho from the pack and put my head through the center hole to cover both me and the pack so that everything would stay relatively dry. Shortly, the splashing rain changed to a steady downpour, sheets of water that closed the forest in around me. My hair was wet and rain dripped into my eyes so that I had to keep wiping them to see. Water came down through the neck hole of the poncho and snaked cold down my back. My feet and legs were soaked from kicking through the wet brush and the cold, wet jeans flapped around my ankles. I started to look for shelter.

At first I stood under the umbrella of a large spruce, hoping that its thick, plumy clusters of needles would keep the rain off. Warnings about lightning striking people who stand under trees briefly came to mind, but I thought that if lightning hit the one tree I was standing under out of the thousands of trees in the forest, it had to be because my number was up anyhow.

The sheltered place under the spruce didn't offer much real protection. Water collected on the branches until its weight canted the clusters of needles, and it rode down the slopes to cascade down on my head. Instead of being rained on steadily in drops, I was being slopped with rain in quantity, as if someone were throwing buckets on me from a second-story window. Peering through the haze of rain, looking for a better spot, I saw a long rock ledge with an overhang cut into the side of the canyon not far from where I was standing. Deciding it might be better shelter, I ducked my head against the rain and climbed up to it. It was an improvement. The rock overhang jutted out far enough to keep out the slanting rain.

I took off my poncho, shook off as much rain as I could, then spread it out to dry. The pack, placed against the back wall of my shallow cave, made a fine backrest. Sitting there, I looked at the sheets of falling water and thought it was like being behind a waterfall, and I worried a little about trying to walk through the wet forest after the rain stopped.

For most of the day it rained. The real downpour lasted only about thirty minutes, but it was replaced by a steady drizzle that teased by pretending to stop. Each time I would decide it was time to go on, the drizzle would increase just enough to convince me to stay.

To pass the time, I played a mental game I called "Going to the Movies." The rules were simple—I thought of a favorite movie, then tried to remember where I saw it, who saw it with me, what the plot was, and what actors played the important roles. At first I imagined the movies I had seen with Kyle, but when I did, it seemed that he had always been unhappy or sullen about something so that I ended up not paying real attention to the movie, only to him. I switched to the movies I'd seen with my mother and B.J. I was about halfway through *Star Wars*, just at the point where Luke (what was the name of the actor?) was swinging like Tarzan across the chasm in the spaceship, when a movement on the side of the ledge made me reach for the spear. It was an animal. At first I thought it was a wolf, but it was much too small. A coyote? Yes. I'd seen one once in Will Rogers State Park—it had sat boldly on its haunches and watched Dave and me as we picnicked. Now this one moved in under the far end of the ledge without seeing me and shook off the rain with a rousing shake that included even his bushy tail. Then, as he turned his head to survey his surroundings, he saw me and stood stock-still. I sat quietly looking at him. He reminded me of Ginger, B.J.'s dog, a wire-haired mongrel. I almost called the coyote to come over so I could give him a good scratch behind the ears.

He stood, waiting to see what I would do. When I did nothing, he sat down and began to pant quietly, his wide mouth open and turned up at the corners so that he seemed to be laughing to himself. He looked thin. I couldn't help but compare us—we were both unsuccessful hunters waiting out the rain, we were both hungry, we were both cold, and we were both thin. Staring at each other, we sat in silent companionship for a while. Then I couldn't resist saying, "Are you down to your last piece of bacon bar, too?" Though I had spoken softly, he ducked out from under the ledge at the sound of my voice and was gone. At once I missed him.

Time passed, and the rain lulled me into quiet contemplation. By early evening, it slowed and stopped. It was too late then to walk any farther and find a campsite by dark, so I decided to stay on the ledge. I unrolled the sleeping bag, undressed, and got into it. I dozed fitfully as darkness moved in, and listened to the sound of water dripping from tree branches. It was a sound I had heard on my first night in the woods, when, frightened, I had wondered if Martha would come and when the rescuers would arrive. How different I feel now, I thought. I no longer look for Martha and I am on my own, on my way out. If I had known what walking out would be like, would I have set out from that first camp? I decided the answer was yes. The reality of what I was going through was nowhere near as bad as my fears of the unknown on that first rainy night.

The next morning, the ankle was healed enough so that I decided to get an early start and try to cover a lot of ground. Ignoring my hunger, I pushed on steadily through the damp woods, telling myself that I would take a long rest at the first clearing.

There weren't any all day.

Chapter Thirteen

That night, after I made camp, I went fishing, but the heavy rain had turned the river muddy and the fish weren't biting. After an hour of catching nothing, I filled the cooking pot with rain water—clearer than the river water—from a depression in a rock along the canyon wall. Then I made a kind of stew from the few berries and ferns I had collected during the day. It left me hungry. Later that night, I took the last tiny piece of bacon bar from the pack and ate it, not taking my time at all and not even relishing the taste. All I wanted was to fill my aching stomach a little more.

The next morning, as I put on the pack, it occurred to me that for the first time I was carrying no food at all. I will have to catch, pick, and/or kill lunch and supper, I thought, but I regarded the idea more with curiosity than fear. By late afternoon, I was not so cocky. The few marshy spots had yielded only a few berries, and when light shining ahead through the tree trunks signaled another open space coming up, I hoped for better pickings.

Before walking into the clearing, I did my standard bear-check number. Staying back in the trees, I looked the space over carefully. Movement. Another flock of ptarmigan. Stepping back behind a large pine, I took off the pack and moved back up to the clearing. The birds had gone uphill and were at the far end. Walking quickly and trying to stay far enough back in the trees to screen myself, I approached the birds, holding the spear ready. Before I could get close enough to try a throw, they moved into the woods above the clearing. I wasn't sure if they had seen me or not. If I watched my footing so as not to make too much noise, maybe I could get closer to them in the woods than in the open spaces. The birds were exasperating, they would move a few paces, stop to eat, picking at the ground, then they would start walking again. Moving with care, I tried to close the distance between me and them. Time after time, I got almost close enough for a shot at one, then they would duck around a tree or behind a log. It was as if a long, invisible arm held me and the birds apart by an uncloseable distance. We climbed into sparser woods and it was harder and harder for me to hide from them.

Finally after I had stalked the birds for nearly an hour, we came to a small, brushy space. The birds went under some brush, out of sight. If they keep moving in the same direction as they have been, I reasoned, then they will appear at the other side of the space. So I loped, almost at a run, around the clearing to cut them off. By the time I had circled around to the other side, I was panting. I crouched behind a small tree, wondering if they had already passed me. No. There they were. Trying to make my breathing shallow to lessen its noise, I watched the first ptarmigan move out from under the brush and toward the trees. Several others followed. Spear ready, I slowly rose. After taking aim at the closest bird, I threw with all my strength. A squawk and a burst of feathers told me the spear had connected. I ran forward and lunged, just as the bird flapped free of the spear. Grabbing with both hands, I pinned it to the ground. With my right hand I reached for the bird's neck. At first it snaked out from under my grasp. I reached again, closed my hand around it. The bird's wings beat in protest. I worked my knife from my belt with my left hand and quickly cut off the bird's head. Blood spurted from the neck, the body jerked several times and then was still.

I was overjoyed. I had done it. Never again would I hurl a javelin into space without feeling kinship with primitive human hunters, who had been killing meat for millions of years. The bird was as large as a small chicken, and my mouth watered in anticipation of supper that night. Picking up the spear and carrying the bird by its scaly feet, I moved down the hill at a near-trot. Then, as the forest became more dense, I slowed up to avoid holes hidden by fallen twigs and leaves and the boobytraps of fallen limbs.

Finally, I could hear the river ahead, but heavy brush and trees hid it from view. Where was the clearing? It was gone. I looked both right and left but couldn't spot the brightness through the trees. Alarm tightened my muscles. Which way? At last, I saw water, gleaming in a band through the trunks of some pines. I was thirsty so I pushed on to drink from the river before trying to decide on an answer to the question of where the clearing was. The river was flowing rapidly over its boulder-strewn bed, shallower now that it had widened. I washed the bird's blood off my hands and drank. Which way? As I crouched there, I cleaned the ptarmigan and sent my mind back over the ground I had covered in the hunt. Where had I gone wrong? I couldn't discover my mistake. The bird's entrails were out, and, kicking a hole first, I buried them. My mind continued its travels—the birds and I had moved first uphill, then—down river? It made sense. I could be downstream from the clearing. But how far downstream? The question, I realized, was ridiculous. The clearing where I'd found the birds was too big to miss. I wouldn't be able to walk by it without seeing it. I'd just have to backtrack for a half hour or so.

Deciding to leave the feathers on the bird until I got to camp, I picked it up, stood, took the spear (which was leaning against a tree), and started off. There was a feeling of freedom in being without the pack—that perpetual burden on my back—and I walked along jauntily, swinging the dead bird like a feather duster.

But the longer I walked, the more apprehensive I became. Had I gone this far chasing the birds? There was no way I could have missed the clearing, was there? I paused by a stream that was no more than a trickle winding its way downhill through the rocks. I made myself stop to drink and rest for a while. The nervousness that urged me on could be dangerous; I knew by now that haste bred mistakes.

"If you can keep your head when all around you are losing theirs ..." Thank you, Mrs. Zimmerman! The remnant of poem made me smile. I couldn't remember any more of it—I'd never been a Kipling fan—but only the annoyance I had felt in class when the poem kept stressing all those "manly" qualities. When I had commented on this in class, Mrs. Zimmerman had smiled and said that Kipling was pretty much untouched by anything close to a feminist viewpoint. Then she'd read us "The Female of the Species" and asked for discussion. As we had hotly debated whether Kipling's contemptible social viewpoint negated the literary quality of his work (questionable), she put her hands behind her head, leaned back in her desk chair, and smiled more broadly.

The message was right, though, I thought—keeping one's head is all important. It calmed me, and I soon got up and started walking again. Finally, far ahead, I could see the clearing. A weight lifted from my spirits and my pace quickened. As I reached the open space, I could see the large tree where I had left my pack. I looked for the patch of blue on the ground, but it wasn't there. Then I was almost across the clearing when I saw the pack moving as if to meet me. I froze. A small black bear had his head halfway inside the pack and, in rooting through it, was scooting it along the ground. Suddenly I was furious. My portable home! My tent, clothes, cooking pot! All about to be torn apart! It was too much. Any fear of the bear turned to rage, and a scream tore itself from deep inside me. "Stop that!" I shouted. "You! Stop it!" The bear jerked his head out of the pack, looked up, saw me coming at him waving the bird, and with one quick snort took off toward the river. Only once did he stop to glance over his shoulder at me before plunging into the water and swimming to the other side, like a fat retriever. Then at once he was lost in the trees.

I stood watching until he disappeared, then burst out laughing. Thinking of the startled expression on the bear's face, I laughed until tears came. "Lisa Gallagher, wild woman of Alaska! The Alaska terror!" I shouted, giving a Tarzan yell of triumph and brandishing the ptarmigan. Then, exuberance abated, I wondered how I would ever convince anyone that I had single-handedly scared off a bear.

I checked the pack and found that everything was still in it, intact; I'd surprised the bear before he could do any damage. For a while I wandered the clearing, scouring it for edibles, and collected almost half a pot full of serviceberries. Greens were in short supply in this part of Alaska, during late summer, Dave's book had told me. The Indians eat several plants in spring, but most of the plants become bitter as they mature, and some even develop what the book called a "poison principle." Whatever that meant, I wasn't about to try eating anything that had it. There was wild celery, and I had seen some, but it was so easy to confuse it with poison water hemlock that I wasn't about to try that, either. I was left looking for Labrador tea (which, "in quantity" could "cause intestinal disturbances") and roseroot, which would probably be a little past its prime.

After I had stashed the berries, there was still enough daylight left to do more walking, and I wanted to get moving to avoid a rematch with the bear. I slipped into the pack and, carrying the ptarmigan, started out.

When the light started to slant through the trees about an hour later, I had reached the stream where I had stopped to rest before. It seemed like a good place to camp, so I put up the tent and started a fire. Sitting cross-legged by the tent, I picked up the bird to pluck it. When I grabbed a handful of glossy brown feathers and yanked, nothing happened. Feather by feather, then, I said to myself, but even one feather was almost impossible to pull out, though after a minute or so, I did succeed in freeing it. Discouraged, I held the bird in my lap and stared into the fire. It would take forever to pluck the bird at this rate. Then I remembered something I had read about cooking game birds, feathers and all, in clay. The clay, hardened by the fire, would grip the feathers when it was cracked open, but the rest of the bird, then cooked, would emerge bald from its mold. It worked like adhesive on hairy skin.

It won't hurt to try it, I thought, and took the bird down to the stream and coated it with an inch or two of what looked like clay (and was probably mud) from the river bank. Then I brought it back and put it in the coals to cook. As it was roasting, I fished for a while. My luck was good, and I added two small trout to the grill.

Guessing the bird had had plenty of time to cook, I snaked it out of the fire with a stick, cracked the mud ball with a stone, then took the knife and pried the clay open. The bird came out naked and feather-free. Expecting it to be tough, I cut off a piece of breast and chewed it. The bird's free-roving hard life had made it tougher than a supermarket chicken, but it was more tender than the squirrel had been and quite tasty. With it, I ate the fish. I saved the bird bones for soup.

Tucked into the sleeping bag later that night, I grinned up at the few stars I could see through the shadowy tree tops as I remembered the bear and how he had high-tailed it away from me. I felt content.

For the next three days, I walked through the forest, stopping at night to fish and set my traps. I was not able to spear another bird, and the traps yielded nothing, so I lived on fish, berries, fern "bananas," and some roseroot, which I recognized by its thick, fleshy leaves. I'd found the roseroot growing in a niche in the canyon wall. It was a little bitter, but I ate it anyhow. My hunger drove me on, along with the conviction that I was getting close to civilization. The river was very wide now, so wide that I could not have crossed it.

On the second and third days, the going became very rough. The dense brush grew high, so that I had to part it with my hands and step through it. My hands and arms were covered with scratches, and my long hair kept getting caught on twigs, so that I had to stop and disentangle it. Three times I came to huge clearings of muskeg too marshy to cross, and walked around them, super-alert for the sound of the river, slapping off the mosquitoes that collected in clouds around me. By now I was rationing the insect repellent, and the mosquitoes zeroed in on me, whining in my ears, landing on my face and hands to bite.

I played the Movie Game to keep from getting bored, going back to old 1940s films I'd seen on television—*Mrs. Miniver, Watch on the Rhine*—movies about people muddling through, being brave. Stiff-upper-lip movies. Once *Snow White* came to mind as I fought my way through a thicket, but I switched my mind from animated malevolent forests to one of the Shakespeare sonnets Mrs. Zimmerman had made us memorize. When my hair got caught again, yanking my head back, I stopped to braid it and tie it with a piece of parachute line. It kept loosening up—braids need elastic bands—so I had to keep stopping to rebraid it.

That third night since the ptarmigan, I tried combing my hair, considering solutions to the braid problem. There was really only one—to cut the hair off. I should think about it, I said to myself, but I was tired and impatient. I took the knife and sawed away at the long plait, cutting it a few strands at a time. The braid was very thick, but I finally held it like a tail in my hand. I had been growing my hair since I was ten, but for some reason, I didn't feel emotional about cutting it off. I dropped the braid into the stream, and watched it as it bobbed along, then slowly sank under the surface. Good riddance, I thought.

The next day, a flock of wild ducks flew overhead, going south, and the brush thinned out so that walking was easier. I was following what seemed like a natural trail that afternoon, enjoying my sudden freedom of movement, watching dust motes dance in the shafts of light that came down through the columnar trees, when I saw something shine on the ground about a yard away from my foot. I leaned over to pick up the bright thing, then realized with a shock what it was—a tiny piece of aluminum foil. I turned it over in my hands, wondering what human package it had come from. A stick of gum? A food pouch? Dazed, I whispered to myself, "People." Human hands had touched the foil, thrown it down. With a whoop, I called, "Hey! Hey, there!" but there was no answer. I had not really expected one. The piece of foil didn't look new, had obviously been laying on the ground for a while. I searched the spot for another human sign, but there was none.

Not knowing why, I put the foil in my jacket pocket and continued on, more eager than ever to cover ground. Someone, another person, had walked this river bank—maybe two days ago, maybe as much as a year ago. And if one person had come this way, it was likely another would, too.

A day later I had come upon no other signs of human beings. When I began to doubt what I had seen, I took the foil from my pocket and looked at it to reassure myself. It was real, about an inch across at its widest place, triangular with two even sides and the third torn. A corner of something. I put the foil back in my pocket, leaned on my spear, and listened. The river roared on, and the wind moaned in the trees. Nothing. I wondered what my rescuers would think of me—a wild-looking person, very dirty, with a jagged mat of filthy hair.

I found a place to sit, overlooking the water, and checked the pack flap—25 marks—. Then I practiced what I would say when I came upon a logger or camper or forest ranger. "Hello, I'm Lisa Gallagher. Twenty-five days ago, I parachuted out of a plane. . . ." I made the speech out loud, listening to my voice as I spoke, and smiled. The rescuers would expect a smile.

Chapter Fourteen

On the following day, I had been on the trail about two hours when I stopped to rest where a small stream formed a large, deep pool that opened out into the river. The sky was overcast, and a cold wind whipped up the narrow river valley. As it whistled through the trees, it sounded like heavy surf hissing toward shore.

When I knelt to drink, out of habit I studied the soft, damp earth by the water's edge. At first I didn't identify what was before my eyes because it was so unexpected. Then it registered. A footprint, the patterned thread engraved deep into the dark earth. I could even read the letters imprinted in mirror image in the six-sided outline in the print's middle—URD. At first I wondered if the print might be mine, knowing it couldn't be. It was too large.

I put my foot beside it and saw that it was at least four inches longer than mine. Then to make doubly sure, I took off one of my boots and studied the bottom. The pattern of the tread on the rubber sole was entirely different, and the brand, too, was not the same.

Now sure, I let my feelings rise to the surface—another human being, more people, food, houses, telephones, home! I leaped to my feet and shouted, jumping up and down in excitement, then realized I had one shoe on and one shoe off. No matter. I shouted again. The wind tore in the words from my mouth.

Quickly I put the boot back on and searched along the river bank for more signs, and immediately found them. Almost at the river's edge were several more boot prints and a place that had been flattened by something heavy being dragged up on the bank. It had to be a boat. The ground held a story—or part of a story. Two different sets of boot prints told me that there were two men. Both were heavy, because the prints sank deep in the ground. The men had been in this place quite recently because the fine, thin ridges around the footprint indentations were sharp and damp; time had not eroded them, and they had been made after the rain.

I was too happy with what I had found to spend much time congratulating myself on my detective work. I shouted again, hoping the men were near enough to hear me, but there was no answer. Standing right on the edge of the river, I craned my neck to look up and down the rushing band of water. It flowed straight south for a while, then—gray under a gray sky—disappeared around a bend. The river was empty, and my search for movement, color, any sign that the men were near yielded nothing. I could feel my blood pounding in my ears as

I thought, they're around here somewhere, I know they are!

Who were the two men? Probably hunters or fishermen, I decided. There was no way to tell which way they had gone or how long they would be away, *if* they were coming back. I waited for a while, sitting on the ground near the footprints, but my excitement—the adrenalin rushing through my bloodstream—kept mounting, telling me to move, and staying put was torture. Better to start walking again, I told myself. If nothing else, it will help burn off my nervous energy.

Stepping quickly along, I tried to stay close enough to the river so that I could keep it in view. I didn't want the men in their boat to get past me. But hours went by, and there was no further sign. Where were they? They must have gone the other way or are ahead of me, I thought. Though I was disappointed, I didn't give up on the idea of finding them. The river was like a road. No one—particularly someone in a canoe—would go far away from it. And if the men had gone upstream, they would be coming back down—sometime.

After all, I said to myself, working my way around a thicket, Robinson Crusoe didn't find Friday until long after he saw the footprint on the beach. Thank you, Mrs. Zimmerman! I smiled, remembering those Friday afternoons when she read us *Robinson Crusoe*, in weekly installments.

Heartened, I walked part of that day, then camped in a clearing overnight, my senses keen, always alert for the sound of a voice or a paddle dipping in the water or an engine humming. It won't be long now, I told myself, fingering the piece of foil and making up speeches to say when I got home.

The next day, the sun came out from behind the clouds for a while, then retreated again. As I fished the river and cooked the two trout I'd caught, I imagined scenes of how it might be when I found the men. Perhaps I'd spot a plume of smoke from their morning campfire. I'd walk up, and tell my story as I drank the hot coffee they would offer me. Or perhaps they would be coming down the river and I'd wave from the bank, then watch as the canoe veered and came toward me.

Quickly I packed up and hit the trail, and walked all morning before anything happened. All the while, I rehearsed, "Hello, I'm Lisa Gallagher . . ." I was nearing the end of my goal, and I felt the satisfaction of accomplishing something difficult. It was as if I'd been in a race. A few more steps, and I'd break the ribbon.

A loud report made me jump. A gunshot! They *were* hunters! They were close; the sound of the gunshot had been loud. At a near-run, I rushed toward the place the sound of the shot had come from. As I ran, breaking through thickets, jumping rocks, I shouted, "Help! Help! Wait!" The roar of the wind, still rushing through the trees, masked the sound of my voice. Through the branches, I saw movement on the other side of the water—a flash of silver. Rushing to the bank of the river, I looked across. A long, metal canoe was beached there. Beside it, a fat man with a heavy red beard was bending over another man sprawled on the ground. It looked as if the second man were hurt. An accident? A hunting accident?

"Hello!" I yelled.

At the sound of my shout, the bearded man jerked upright. I waved as I shouted, "Help! Over here!"

It was not as I had rehearsed. The fat man did not answer me, but stood there staring. He was wearing a green plaid jacket.

"Is your friend hurt?" I shouted. "Can I help?"

The bearded man jumped over to crouch beside the canoe and jerked something from his belt. It was a pistol. His actions startled me. The only thing I could think of was that I had somehow frightened him by appearing out of nowhere.

"It's all right. I need help!" I yelled. I couldn't think of anything else to say.

For a moment, I stood on the river bank. The bearded man crouched, pointing his pistol at me, and the other man lay limp on the ground. It was like Statues, the game you play in grade school. I was frightened. Something was terribly wrong. In none of my rehearsals had there been anything like this.

Then I saw blood on the fallen man's shirt, a large dark patch of blood, slowly spreading. I had opened my mouth to say something about it, when the bearded man's voice boomed across the water. "Who are you?"

"Lisa Gallagher," I said. "My name is Lisa Gallagher. Twenty-seven days ago, I parachuted..."

He interrupted me. "Who's with you?" Still holding the gun menacingly, he stood.

Before I could answer, the man on the ground moved. The bearded man jumped toward him, and I knew he was going to hit the fallen man. Without thinking, I screamed, "Don't!"

At my shout, the attacker ordered, "You shut up and stand there. Don't move." I was all wrong. Maybe it was a hallucination. People alone too long have hallucinations, I thought. I felt as if I had somehow stumbled into a horror movie. In the frame of the trees and underscored by the gray river, the two men and the canoe, as if in a picture, seemed to be objects I could erase with a turn of mind. I tried by an act of will to wipe them out of my field of vision. They stayed. They were real.

As the bearded man again bent over his companion, I started edging away from the bank. He looked up and saw I had changed my position. "I said for you to stand still!" Momentarily, I stopped moving, but my mind was racing. Whatever it was that had happened here, I didn't want to be part of it. It all reeked of danger. The forest was safe. This scene wasn't. These people weren't. When the bearded man again glanced down at the man on the ground, he gave me the moment I needed. I dodged behind a tree, spun around, and started racing away from the river. I heard a shout, followed by the report of the gun. The bullet cracked through the branches over my head. I ducked low, glancing back to keep trees between us so he couldn't get a clear shot. Fear gave me energy. Another explosion of the gun; it was muffled by distance. Concentrating, I picked a path for my flying feet. At any moment, I expected something to smash between my shoulder blades. Was he chasing me? I couldn't hear anything, but I didn't stop to listen, and kept running, low and fast, choosing the thickest parts of the forest as cover.

I was looking behind me, when my foot hit something soft and plunged into it, throwing me off balance, so that I fell headlong into a bog, hidden by brush. Panting with fear, I pulled my way up out of it. In the moment before I started running again, I listened, but heard nothing. Then, more careful to pick the way ahead, I began speeding along again. Every time my feet hit the ground, there were sloshing sounds.

After a few moments, I heard a distant scraping —metal against rock—that told me Red Beard was launching the canoe. I didn't look back, but ran faster. I tried to guess what he would do. Head me off down river? Chase me through the trees? Forget me? What? Pausing behind a tree to catch my breath, gulping air, I tried to make some decisions. Should I drop the pack? If I did, I'd be able to move faster. No, I thought immediately, keep it. Throw it away only as a last resort. Without the sleeping bag, I could freeze to death in the nights, which were getting colder as fall came, and I had no idea how long I would be in the woods. Particularly now. Particularly if I was being hunted.

Leaning against the tree, I strained to listen over the sound of my heavy breathing. I heard nothing. Looking around the tree, I saw that I had covered enough distance so that the river was no longer visible through the trees. Still staying low as possible, I started moving again. Steadily I worked my way up the mountainside. Trying to keep from leaving signs of where I had been, I avoided walking on bare earth and tried to break as few twigs as possible. The trees became sparse as I climbed higher, and I began to worry about not having enough cover. Someone with binoculars might be able to see me, or at least the blue of my pack, as I climbed upward. Just as I was getting very nervous, darting from tree to tree, I saw a dense willow thicket.

I pushed through into its center and dropped my pack and spear. The branches and leaves were taller than I, and the world outside was hidden from me, so I knew I was safe. I sat down and surveyed the damage from my fall in the bog. The front of my jacket was damp, but it was slick enough so the water hadn't penetrated to its inside. My jeans were muddy, but I had another pair. The boots would dry out. I looked down at my hands—the mud was starting to dry and crack—and suddenly the enormity of what had happened broke through to me. I was overcome with fear. My teeth started to chatter, and I tried to hold my shaking body still.

Try to make some sense out of it! Don't fall apart! I told myself sternly. What had happened? Maybe I had gone crazy? No. Impossible. My head had never been clearer. What I had seen had not been a hallucination. It had been too real, had gone on too long. Scenes from old movies crowded into my mind. While I had been alone in the woods, something weird had happened to the world. Everyone was crazy but me; aliens had dropped an evil gas into the air to drive us all out of our heads so they could take over Earth. Or I had walked through a time machine into the Old West. No, the canoe was metal. Stop, I said to myself. Stop right here. What has happened is that by some wild chance I have stumbled onto a criminal—a killer? He knows that I saw him. He may or may not come after me, depending on how dangerous he thinks I am or how closely he's being pursued. If he's being pursued, then other people are in this woods, people I can trust. But maybe he's part of a gang. If he is, other people may be my enemies. How can I tell them apart? The friends and enemies?

It was all too bizarre for me to accept, though I knew it was true. Somewhere in that woods was

Red Beard. . . . Maybe he was coming for me now. Suddenly I felt closed in, jailed, by the thicket because I couldn't see out. Maybe he was standing out there on its edge. . . . I crawled slowly and silently to the edge of the thicket on my belly. Nothing. Several times I held my breath to listen for the sound of someone moving through the trees farther down the slope. Nothing. The forest was silent and still. The wind had gone down, and nothing moved.

Then, a faint hum. I cocked my head in its direction to listen. It grew louder. A plane! I saw it flying low, over the river. Was it friends of Red Beard? I wanted to leap up and wave, but the vision of what had happened on the river bank held me back. I no longer automatically associated things human with help. They seemed just as likely to mean danger. Then the plane was gone. The noise of the engine died away. It dawned on me—days and days of walking to find civilization, and the first human being I see is a killer! I lowered my head on my muddy arms and sobbed quietly.

After a few minutes, I stopped. I didn't want to give in to it. Looking up at the sky, I whispered, "If I just keep going, everything will turn out all right." I wished there were more conviction in my voice.

As time passed and the light started to fade, I started to plan what I would do. I couldn't travel at night, so it seemed best to stay hidden in the willow thicket until first light, then move down river as fast as I could. Before it got too dark to see, I unrolled the sleeping bag. If it started to rain, I'd pull the poncho over me and try to stay as dry as I could. Taking off my wet clothes and boots, I changed into dry socks, shirt, and jeans, then crawled into the sleeping bag. For a long time, I lay in the dark, eyes open, then dozed off into uneasy sleep.

All night, I kept jerking awake in terror as the cruel face of Red Beard loomed up in my restless dreams. Once, toward morning, when the dream came again, I woke and thought with relief—that's it, the whole thing is a dream. It has to be. Things like shootings on river banks don't happen in real life. It was too much of a coincidence for to have seen what I had seen. But my mind slowly came back to the truth. If it hadn't happened, why was I here in the thicket? How did I get there? I felt the crusty mud still on my hands, now dried, and reality crushed down on me. "Sleep, don't think about it now," I told myself. I knew I needed to rest.

Sleep didn't come. I watched the sky above me slowly turn from black to gray. After putting on my damp boots over the dry socks, I quickly rolled the sleeping bag and got ready to go. I hated to leave the thicket to expose myself to danger. As I put on my nearly dry jacket and the pack, the thought that had always been in the back of my mind pushed into my consciousness: "What if he's waiting?" The image of Red Beard, leaning against his tree, a mean smile on his face, gun in hand, waiting for me to come out of the thicket, made my hand tremble as I picked up the spear. Fearfully, I slowly stood up and quickly worked my way out of the thicket into the open forest. I saw nothing but trees on all sides and heard nothing but the wind, now quieter than the day before.

I decided when I began walking that I'd stay just far enough away from the river so that I knew where it was, but not so close that I would risk running into Red Beard. As I trudged along, I stopped to listen every few minutes and to try to peer ahead through the trees for movement. Finally, as I saw and heard no one, the fear that had knotted my stomach eased, and hunger and thirst took its place. I kept going, not knowing if I was walking toward danger or safety.

Chapter Fifteen

All that day, I walked up on the ridges, staying in the dense stands of trees where I would be hidden but could keep an eye out for Red Beard. When I stopped to drink from the feeder streams, I looked around on the ground for traces of him, but there were none and I was glad.

In my mind, as I threaded through the trees, I kept going over and over the conversation I had had with the man, with the river separating us, and I tried to find another interpretation of what had happened. Was I wrong to think he had shot his partner? Was there any other explanation? Might I have run away from nothing? But, no. The bullets that had whizzed over my head were real. Maybe his partner (if that's who the fallen man was) was just wounded. Should I have stayed to keep Red Beard from killing him? But I had no weapon, and Red Beard would just have killed me, too.

To get the murderous scene out of my head, I tried to remember the words of the poems Mrs. Zimmerman had taught us. By now I knew all of

"Psalm of Life," parts of "The Ancient Mariner," and a little Kipling. When I ran out of poems, I silently ran through songs we had sung on the bus on school field trips—"Ninety-nine Bottles of Beer on the Wall" was the best, because it lasted the longest. Then I hummed "Oh Shenandoah," my father's favorite, under my breath. When I got to the line "I long to see you," I felt tears come into my eyes.

No matter what I did, I couldn't sink into a steady walking rhythm as I had before I'd seen Red Beard. Every time I would start to swing along with the beat of my own walking, my brain would jerk me out of it, shouting danger, and I'd search the open spaces between the columns of tree trunks for him and stop to listen.

That night I made a dry camp in a dense stand of brush. Sleeplessness, lack of food, and fear had made me nervous, so I didn't sleep well. I missed having a fire.

The next day, I came awake quickly from a doze thinking I smelled smoke from a campfire—Red Beard's?—but I couldn't tell if I was imagining it or not. I unzipped the sleeping bag and stood (I had slept in my clothes), turning in a circle to scan the woods for smoke, but I saw none, and the faint smell, if it had existed at all, seemed to drift away.

I felt shaky and lightheaded and wondered to myself how long I could go without food. "As long as I have to," my mind answered. "Okay, let's look at the thing. That nut may be chasing me. Maybe not. But I can't take a chance because he shoots at people. And I can do *something* about food. Fish in the small streams. Set snares. Eat the meat raw if I catch any. It's too risky to start a campfire." The thought of Red Beard standing between me and my food supply—I really wanted to fish the river, but didn't dare because I'd make too good a target—filled me with sudden rage. Who did Red Beard think he was, anyway? Just because he had a gun . . .

I put on the pack, and it felt heavier than usual. As I set out, I realized that my nerves were shot. My eyes kept darting anxiously as I checked every slight movement, and I felt a cold, inward shaking as I trudged through the dense brush, tripping over logs hidden under leaves and just barely catching myself before I'd fall.

Toward mid-morning, I came to a clearing and stood on its edge, heart beating fast. I saw spots of red—cranberries?—but at first was afraid to move into the open space. Then I edged my way in. As I picked the berries, I felt exposed, as if Red Beard, hidden behind a tree, had me centered in his gunsights. At any moment I expected a bullet to come zapping out of the dark forest from behind me.

My jeans were slipping, so I retied my nylon-line belt, gathering them around the waist. As I did, I noticed that my bootlace was becoming untied, so I leaned down to fix it. The lace was badly frayed, about to break. I walked to the far edge of the clearing, took off my pack, and rummaged in it for another piece of line. When I tried to cut it for a lace, my hand was shaking so much that I had to take the line, lay it on a log, position the knife, and cut that way. It took a long time for me to put in the new lace and tie up the boot.

When I stood, I looked toward the river and for an instant was sure I saw a canoe, then realized that from where I was I couldn't see the river at all and that the "canoe" was two branches at a certain angle. It was like one of those puzzles in a children's magazine, the kind in which cats and faces are hidden in pencil drawings of scenes.

My mind is playing tricks on me, I said to myself, and walked on. About an hour later, as I skirted a marshy spot, I noticed that some twigs on the brush were freshly broken off—the wood inside the bark at the broken places was white and raw. Red Beard? He could have come through here! And then again, I answered myself, it could have been a moose or a bear or another person.

Not long after, I heard splashing from the direction of the river, then the rhythmic, liquid sound of a canoe paddle dipping in the water. Choosing spots for my feet, I stole closer to the river and found a gap in the branches through which I could get a view of the water. The trees were thick, and I was sure whoever it was wouldn't be able to see me.

Then the front of the canoe, a flash of silver, nosed out into my framed view, followed by the orange-red beard and the green plaid jacket. Red Beard. It was all I needed. I melted back into the forest, sick with despair. He *did* exist. I *hadn't* imagined him. He was going the same way I was— toward the ocean and civilization. Why? If he were a fugitive, wouldn't he be headed upstream, not downstream? I played with the answers, as I leaned against a tree. Maybe he figured the heat was off. Maybe he was meeting someone somewhere to get supplies.

With the questions turning over and over in my mind, I pushed farther into the woods, away from the river. I walked as softly as I could, and I tried to disturb the underbrush as little as possible.

Sometimes I saw movement from the corner of my eye, would jerk my head around to look, and find nothing there. It was as if something was following me, swishing into the underbrush when I turned, but watching me all the time.

Finally evening came, and the light slanted through the trees. I was looking forward to darkness because it would give me more cover. I had just stepped over a log, when I looked up and saw a flash of green plaid very clearly ahead of me. I stopped still, looked again. It was gone. Maybe he was behind a tree. Not moving, I waited, staring into the forest, then the green plaid began to form before my eyes again, coming out of the pattern of tree branches and willow leaves, the low-slanting light. I *was* seeing things.

The experience didn't frighten me, though it made me anxious. I knew what it came from—fatigue, hunger, and fear. Now I knew I had to get something to eat and a good night's rest. For the thousandth time, I started walking again, and when I came to the next small stream, which tumbled down over smooth rocks, I unrolled my fish line, tied it to my spear, baited it with a bug I found by the water, and threw it in the water. It was not a good place for fishing—the water was too shallow and rapid. In an hour, I had caught nothing, so I quit.

After making camp in a thicket, I set my snares. Then I got into the sleeping bag and tried to doze off. Just as sleep was coming, a sound brought me awake. My heart was pounding in terror. The sound came again. Fully awake now, I realized what it was—an owl, somewhere in a tree above me. Lying there, I was comforted by the soft sound of the owl's call, and I drifted off to sleep until dawn. When it came, I got up, checked the snares, expecting and finding nothing, then set off again.

All that morning I walked. Once I thought I heard a shout, and another time a face formed out of the bark of a tree trunk, then faded away. I didn't see Red Beard or hear him or find signs that he had been where I was.

Early in the afternoon, I spotted a clearing through the trees. As I got closer, I could see that it was a large one. At the top of it, up next to the tree line, was a log cabin. Real? It seemed solid and three-dimensional and as I stood, staring at it and shifting the weight of my pack, it stayed where it was and didn't fade or disappear. Is it *his* cabin, I wondered. Is he in there? Moving well back from the open space, I worked my way through the woods up to the part of the clearing where the cabin was.

Finally, I was as close as I dared go. The cabin looked deserted. I could see that the windows were dirty; one was cracked—and that the door was closed. For a long time, I studied the stovepipe sticking up above the roof for traces of smoke. Nothing. If Red Beard was in there, he was not letting anyone know he was. I sat down where I could see the clearing.

All that afternoon and evening, I stayed back in the trees watching the cabin. From where I was, I could see a raw spot over in the side of the mountain—digging. Whoever lived in the cabin was a miner. Red Beard didn't seem the type to be a miner.

At sunset, I took off my pack and, leaving my

spear next to it, crawled closer to the cabin to see if I could hear anything. There was no sound. As it got dark, no lights were lit inside. Just before it got too dark to see, I went back to my pack and silently stole back to a small stream I had noticed before to spend the night. Before falling asleep, I decided that in the morning I would try to get into the cabin to search for food. I was sure now that the cabin didn't belong to Red Beard. And if he were hiding out from the law, he wouldn't go to a place as obvious as the cabin. So I convinced myself that checking out the cabin would be relatively safe.

Toward morning, I looked up and watched the stars fade and the sky lighten. Before the sun was up, I was back at the edge of the clearing. Pausing for a moment, I surveyed the whole scene—the clearing, the cabin, and the river bank below. There was no sign of any change from the day before. If Red Beard had left the canoe at the river, he had hidden it. I decided to be doubly safe and check the edges of the clearing for footprints and broken branches. It took me close to an hour to circle it in the trees. Nothing. And during that whole hour, the cabin had been silent, and no smoke came from its chimney.

Finally, placing my pack against a tree and taking the spear, I started to enter the clearing. It seemed as if a thousand eyes watched me over a thousand gun barrels as I walked toward the cabin. For some reason, I felt it was important not to run. My teeth were clenched so tightly that my jaws ached by the time I reached the cabin door. Without pausing, I reached for the door knob, my heart in my throat, and twisted. The door swung open. Every muscle tense, I peered inside. It was empty! I stepped through the door and quickly looked around. A table, two chairs, and a bunk built against the wall furnished the place. The table top was thick with dust. Cupboards lined the wall next to an old woodstove. A discolored piece of cardboard was nailed to one of the cupboard doors. On it, scrawled print read, "Vein played out in the mine. Headed back to Kake. This is still my cabin. Grub in the end cupboard if you need it." The note was signed "Jesse Lattimore."

I jerked open the cupboard door. Bright-colored labels stared back at me; the shelves were lined with canned goods. Just as I reached for a can of Spam, a movement at the window made me leap with fear. I turned and saw it was a bird, standing on the wide windowsill outside and pecking at something. To be sure it was the bird that had caught my eye, I walked to the window to check the clearing. Looking out through the filthy glass, I realized that I felt trapped in the cabin.

Quickly I went back to the cupboard and picked out an armful of food, then saw a can opener on the bottom shelf. I put the food down on the dusty table and went back to the shelves to get the can opener, which I put in my jacket pocket. Then I picked the food up again and went out. I was careful to leave everything as it was, but I noticed I had left footprints in the dust on the floor and a bare spot on the table where I'd put the cans down.

My reluntance to run was gone, and I sped back to the cover of the forest. Kneeling down by the pack, I stuffed the cans inside, then, carrying the pack by a strap, I hurried back to the stream. I could hardly control my shaking as I examined my treasure—three cans of Spam, two of tuna, two of chicken soup, and a large one of peaches.

An hour later, I sat with my back against the tree, full of Spam and peaches, my hunger satisfied for the first time in weeks. With the food came better spirits. I told myself I'd go back to the cabin to get more cans, then travel on. Was Red Beard really Jesse Lattimore? Now I was absolutely certain that the answer to that question was no. The man who had threatened me on the river bank was not the kind who would offer strangers his food. Had Jesse Lattimore taken a boat to Kake? How far away was Kake? After a while the flow of questions slowed and stopped. I opened the other end of the empty cans, stamped them flat, and buried them. Then I headed back to the cabin. I had eaten so much that I was sleepy, but I decided to pick up the food and walk awhile before I slept.

At the cabin, I took only what I thought I needed—five more cans of tuna and Spam, two of beef stew, five of fruit cocktail. The pack was heavy as I shrugged into it. Looking around the cheerful room, I thought, if I stayed here, I could sleep in a real bed tonight. But immediately my imagination painted a scene: I am in a deep sleep when the door bursts open, and Red Beard, gun in hand, is standing in the doorway. The picture helped me hurry on my way.

On the other side of the clearing, as I stood in the trees, I surveyed the clearing for what I thought was the last time. It was a beautiful spot. The owner had built the snug little cabin so that it faced the river for the view. I could live in a place like this and be happy, I thought.

Only a few steps into the trees, I stopped to adjust the waist strap on the pack so my hips, rather than my back, would take more of the new weight from the canned goods. I was kneeling down beside the pack when something moving on the river caught my eye. As I watched, a dark canoe moved up toward the clearing from downstream. Two men in the canoe were paddling hard against the current. As they reached the clearing, they moved the canoe in toward the bank.

Chapter Sixteen

Crouched down and dragging my pack, I melted back into the woods where I felt the men in the canoe couldn't see me. From behind a tree I watched them to find out what they do. Before meeting up with Red Beard, I would have gone running to greet them, but now I felt unsure and afraid. The men might be Red Beard's confederates.

The two sat low in the canoe, intently watching the cabin, letting themselves drift sideways into the brush at the side of the clearing. They think someone's in the cabin, I thought, and they don't want to be seen. I wondered if they had been observing me? Was one of them Lattimore? Once they were hidden from the cabin by brush, they quickly leapt from the canoe and splashed ashore, pulling the canoe behind them, then beaching it.

As soon as they were on dry land, they both grabbed rifles from the canoe. The sight of the rifles made me shrink back further into the underbrush. Staying well back against the trees, they started walking on the opposite side of the clearing up toward the cabin. Then they circled up in back of the cabin, and stealthily approached the door, hugging the wall and staying below the windowsills. One man quickly stood and kicked in the door to look inside, then they both disappeared into the cabin.

I thought of running, but decided not to. The idea that they could be friends kept me there watching. The signs I had left in the cabin—footprints in the dust on the floor and a mark in the dust on the table where I had put down the canned goods—would alert them to the fact that someone was around. If they were Red Beard's friends, they probably wouldn't hesitate to kill me.

I waited for what seemed like a long time. A leafy branch beside my head moved slightly as the wind came up a little; it made me jump. I felt cramped crouched behind the tree, but I knew that if I tried to move from my hiding place, they were almost certain to see me if they had come out of the cabin. The world *had* gone crazy. Fighting down the panic that the idea shot through me, I edged my head around the side of the tree where small bushes would hide my face. The two men were less than ten yards away! They were so close I could see what they were wearing—Levi's and blue chambray shirts. They were both about the same height— over six feet, but one was blonde and one was darkhaired. They moved closer. I froze, close to panic. Not fifteen feet from me, they stopped. Then the dark-haired man took a black box from his belt and pulled a silver antenna out of it. A radio.

He started to talk in a low voice. "Mack, this is Jim. Over." The radio crackled a response that I couldn't understand. Jim answered, "Yeah, we're at the old Lattimore cabin. He may have been in there. We could see where someone had walked through the dust. Did you get that report from Juneau yet?" The radio's reply was long, and both men listened attentively. Jim spoke into the radio again. "Well, I don't think it was him in Wrangell. After all the news stories, people are seeing him everywhere. Anybody that sees a guy with a red beard calls in to say he saw Larsen. I'm sure he's around here somewhere. He's holed up here before. Why don't you ask the forest service people if they'll lend us a couple of their planes to check farther up river?" Again, there was a crackling from the radio, then Jim signed off, pushed down the antenna, and returned the black box to his belt.

Now I knew what they were—police or rangers. And they were after Red Beard. Even though I was sure they weren't enemies, I found it hard to move. Finally, summoning up my courage, I said, "Excuse me."

Both men spun around at the sound of my voice, their rifles leveled at the tree I was crouching behind. "It's all right," I said. "I'm on *your* side."

Jim spoke first. "Let's nobody do anything hasty. Just stand up and come out. Slow and easy, please."

I did as he asked and we stared at each other for a few moments. Then the blond man asked, "Who are you?" as they both lowered their rifles.

His question triggered a flood of words from me. In a rush, I told them who I was and what had happened—the crash, the walking, Red Beard. It sounded nothing like my careful rehearsals, and came out in a jumble, but I knew by their nods that they understood what I was saying. They had obviously heard about my disappearance. As I finished, they walked over to me.

Jim said, "Well, Lisa, you're all right now. You've had enough close calls to last you for a while."

I nodded an emphatic yes, then asked, "Who's the man you're after?"

"Larsen's his name, and as you guessed, he's on the wrong side of the law," Jim answered. "He and the guy with him robbed a bank two, maybe three weeks ago. They must have had a falling out about the time you ran across them. Some of our people found his partner, Richards, where Larsen left him. He's in bad shape, but he'll make it." Then he added, "Why don't you sit down and relax. I'll get a plane in to fly you out." He pulled the radio from his belt. While he was making arrangements, I thought, dazed, I'm going home! I'll be back with them all—with Mother, B.J., Dave—maybe tomorrow. I was smiling.

I thought Jim's smile as he replaced the radio was a reflection of mine, but he turned and said, "Just one request, Lisa."

"What's that?"

He nodded toward his blond partner as he answered, "You've got to promise not to tell anybody how high Greg and I jumped when you said, 'Excuse me!' from behind that bush!"

Soon we were all laughing.

The plane had been the same one I had heard flying overhead a few days before. While we waited for it to come, I gave Jim and Greg the details of my run-in with Larsen. As I related the story, again

I saw the metal canoe, the man lying wounded on the ground, Larsen's red beard, his sudden move for his gun.

"You were lucky to get away with a full hide," Jim commented. He had been watching my face as I told my story.

Greg added, "And Richards told us enough so the two of them will be locked up for a long time."

Feeling suddenly tired from all the excitement, I sat on the ground and leaned my back against a tree, my pack and spear within arm's length.

Jim changed the subject. "You're from Los Angeles, aren't you? That's what the report said when your plane went down."

"Yes, and smog or no smog, it will look good to me."

"You must have done a lot of camping and backpacking," Jim said. "Or else you wouldn't have come through this as well as you did."

"No, I was on my way to join my Dad for my first backpacking trip when all this happened. I wasn't even looking forward to it that much."

Both men shook their heads in amazement, and Ted commented, "Well, you can sure say you're an expert backpacker now. Martha was afraid you were a goner, for sure, after two weeks went by and you weren't found. But she didn't give up on you."

"You know Martha? What happened to her?"

Jim hunkered down beside me. "She got out of the plane okay, and was found about a week later. Ever since, whenever she's had a free day, she's joined in the flying search for you." He paused a moment, then said, "Why don't you relax while Greg and I plan our next move?"

"Sure," I said. I was grateful that the conversation wasn't focused on me any more. I needed a little time to myself. I watched the two men, gesturing as they discussed their moves. Besides Larsen and Richards, they were the first people I had seen in weeks. I was hearing English spoken in voices other than my own, and it sounded a little strange. Yet I was very happy.

The radio crackled, and Jim took it from his belt to talk to the pilot of the plane, who was asking for further directions. Seeing the radio, I had a sudden thought. "My folks don't know I'm safe," I said to Jim. "Is there any way you can radio them?"

Jim hit his head in dismay. "Sorry I didn't think of it before. The excitement, I guess. But, sure. I'll radio Lamar to call ahead to Juneau." Jim began to speak into the radio. I relaxed and lay back, moving my pack under me as a kind of pillow for my back, by now an old habit. As I did, I felt the sharp edges of the cans. "I should put these canned goods back in the cabin," I said. "They do belong to the man who owns it."

"Lattimore," said Greg.

"Yes, he left a note. Do either of you know him?" I stood and stretched.

"I saw old Jesse last week in Wrangell," said Jim, as the two men stood too and the three of us walked up to the cabin. "Why?"

"If you see him, would you please tell him thanks from me—for the food, I mean? I'd like to leave some money for what I ate, too." I took the cans from the pack, then reached in the pocket for my money, which suddenly had value again.

At the sight of the bills in my hand, Greg shook his head. "You'd hurt his feelings if you offered him money. But I'll pass your thanks along."

I found myself staring down at the money—it looked artificially green.

"Being back in civilization takes some getting used to, doesn't it, Lisa?" asked Jim, smiling. He leaned against the cupboard doors.

Nodding, I began to pick up the cans to put them back on the shelves, along with the can opener, and said, "Tell me about Lattimore."

The two started to talk about Lattimore's mine and how it had never produced very much, just enough to keep old Jesse in groceries. After I finished putting the cans on the shelf, I sat in one of the chairs. It was the first chair I had been in since Juneau, and it felt strange to sit, with my legs bent at the knees so they were at right angles to the floor, my back against a piece of flat wood. Things seemed complicated, everything was happening too fast. There had been so much to think about—letting my folks know I was okay, wondering about money, explaining myself. In the woods, I'd thought of things one at a time -- catching a fish, setting a snare, planning a trail.

Listening with part of my mind to the Lattimore story as Jim, still leaning against the cupboards, told how Jesse, an old man now, came down into Wrangell a couple of times a year to buy food and other supplies, I started to relax. In spite of the fact there was a lot to think about, still I didn't have to worry any more about bears or getting food or where I was going. I started to yawn.

Jim laughed. "Guess I'm not much of a storyteller."

"Oh, no, it's really very interesting," I said, before I realized he was teasing.

It was then that we heard the sound of the approaching plane. The noise of the droning engine grew louder as we left the cabin and walked to the river's edge, where the plane splashed down to a landing, its broad pontoons slapping the water as it coasted to a stop. As the plane turned and bore down on us, I must have shrunk away from the noise—loud and unfamiliar, almost frightening—for Jim, sensing what I felt, put a gentle hand on my shoulder and said, "After I've been out in the woods a while, coming back always makes me jumpy at first."

I smiled, glad that he understood. I hadn't realized how much I'd missed human understanding until then. The pilot cut the engine. In the sudden lack of loud noise, I was again aware of the wind moaning high in the trees around the clearing and of the sound of the river rushing toward the sea.

The plane coasted into the bank. Jim introduced me to the pilot, a tall, balding man, who was just completing his leap from the bobbing pontoon to the safety of the shore. "This is Lamar Fitzgerald, Lisa," he said. "Lamar, this is Lisa Gallagher -- the girl that had to parachute out of the M&R plane last month."

Lamar, with a quick, impish smile, shook my hand and said, "Most people figured you were buzzard bait by now. You don't look much the worse for wear."

I smiled my thanks and asked, "Were you able to tell Juneau I'm here?"

Lamar nodded. "I called up there right away. The main office will tell your Dad. He's in Juneau —just got back two days ago. He and a couple of his friends walked the woods for ten days looking for you. He's been beside himself with worry."

As he talked, he picked up my pack and led the way to the plane. Something was missing. My spear! It was on the ground where my pack had been. I looked back at Jim. "Is it all right to take my . . ." I paused. I didn't know what to call the long stick with its crudely sharpened and fire-hardened point, it seemed silly to call it a spear. Jim reached down and handed it to me. "You bet you'll need this. It's evidence. When your grandkids don't want to believe your Alaska stories, you can whack them with it." He handed it to me as I got into the plane.

As Lamar started the engine, Jim and Greg turned the plane around and pushed us off the bank. Then we taxied for take-off, and I could see the two men getting into their canoe. They both waved, and I waved back. The river narrowed and fell away small below me as the plane rose. For a moment, I remembered flying in the M&R plane over a similar landscape, then the sputtering engine, and I expected to feel the same panic again, but I didn't. For the next hour, I watched the ground go by beneath us. It looked different from the air. I had spent weeks slowly walking through those tall trees, over piles of fallen branches, up and down the canyon, and now we'd fly over it all in less than half an hour. I glimpsed stretches of water below—the Pacific—and later, expanses of bays and green islands. Occasionally, I saw a boat or house, then Juneau. Excitement washed over me. It *was* over. I had done it! Tonight I wouldn't have to look for a campsite or set snares or go fishing. There would be food and hot water and clean sheets. And I'd be with my father.

Chapter Seventeen

Lamar landed the plane smoothly and taxied toward a small dock where several people waited. As we sped closer, I could see Dad in the crowd, craning his neck to catch a glimpse of me. Lamar cut the engine, and when we coasted into the dock, several people shouted hello and two photographers snapped pictures of the plane.

Dad opened the door on my side, and I jumped out into his long arms. His angular, bony body was trembling a little and tears came to my eyes as we embraced. He stepped away to look into my face. "Are you all right, Lisa?"

"I'm fine, Dad. I really am," I said. I was so happy to see his familiar face with its blue eyes like mine, the crows' feet, his long nose, the crescents in the corners of his mouth when he smiled.

Before we could say anything more, the questions started. One of the reporters pushed a microphone at me, and I instinctively shrank back. He said he was from a television station and would I tell the listening audience just what it was like out there. Not knowing what to say, I was silent for a moment, but before I could answer, he went on, "It must have been a terrible experience for you, Miss Gallagher. Wasn't it?" Without pausing for a reply, he continued, "How were you able to survive all those weeks with no food and . . ." My father, who had one arm around me, waved the reporter away with his other arm.

"She needs to rest," my father said. "We'll be at the Baronoff. Maybe after she's had an hour or two to herself, she'll answer some questions. Not now."

The newsmen persisted, crowded around us, but Dad pushed through them. It was like a scene from a movie. Lamar's booming voice carried easily over the sound of the reporters' questions. "Hey, Lisa, what do you want me to do with the bear skin and the dead wolf? They're starting to stink pretty bad." I turned to see him standing on the plane's pontoon, grinning.

"I'll pick them up later," I answered, smiling back.

"And your mosquito collection?"

"That you can keep!" I shouted, as Dad and I moved along the pier and the people pressed around the plane. When we walked away, I heard Lamar saying to a television reporter, "I understand she used a rock to down the bear, but strangled the wolf with her bare hands."

In the car that Dad had rented, we drove toward the hotel. Ahead of us were huge steel and concrete buildings. Cars whizzed by. Buses groaned to a stop at corners. It seemed like something from a television science-fiction special. The buildings were incredible; there were large hives of people; the cars and buses moved too fast. It was all too much. The rest of the drive was a blur, with little conversation between Dad and me.

When we went through the hotel lobby, people stopped to stare, and for the first time since I had gotten back among people I wondered what I looked like. The full-length mirror beside the elevator doors gave me my answer. I gasped in shock. The dull tangle of hair, the thin and dirty face, and the filthy clothes seemed to belong to someone else.

Dad caught me looking at myself. "A long soak in the bathtub will do wonders," he said. "You must have lost twenty pounds."

Jokingly, I replied, "That's *one* advantage anyway. I got thin. Without trying."

Dad nodded. "You look great. Still, just to be sure, I've got a doctor waiting to examine you. We'll call your mother first, though—she's been worried sick."

When we got into my room, I threw my pack on the bed. Dad noticed the ink marks on the flap. "What are these?"

"I needed a way to keep track of the days," I said. He turned his head so I wouldn't see his tears.

Mom's voice, when we managed to put through the call to her, was strong but tearful. "Are you all right?" she asked.

I assured her that I was fine. "Except for about twenty missing pounds."

"Oh, Lisa," she said, laughing and crying at the same time.

"And I cut my hair off with my knife. It was getting in the way."

"I can't wait to see you. When will you be coming home?"

"Dad says he's got reservations on a plane tomorrow. We should be in about two-fifteen." It felt odd to be holding a green phone receiver in my hand and talking to Mom, over a thousand miles away.

We talked a little longer. Every once in a while, she would ask again if I was okay, and I would reassure her. When I could tell she was feeling better, I told her again not to worry, said a long good bye, and put the phone back in its cradle.

After the doctor affirmed what I knew was true —that I was in good shape—I went in to take a hot bath. My fingernails were black and broken and my hands scarred and scabbed, but I was happy to be lying in the water, which was like velvet on my skin, scrubbing away at the dirt encrusted on my feet and hands. If I don't get it off, it will wear off, I thought philosophically. With the hotel soap, I washed my ragged mop of hair. Even short, it was snarled so much that I couldn't untangle it, and after a while I rinsed it out and gave up. "I'm supposed to be a wild woman, so I guess I'll look the part," I said out loud.

"What?" came Dad's voice from the other side of the closed door.

I laughed. "Oh, I'm just talking to myself, Dad. It's an old habit from the woods."

I lay back in the tub relaxing, watching the reflection of the water in the white porcelain tub make light ripples on the ceiling. When my skin began to wrinkle, I got out of the tub, dried myself off with the big hotel towel, combed out my hair as best I could, and put on the bathrobe Dad had loaned me.

Dad was waiting with two double-thick milkshakes. I could drink only about half of one of them before I'd had enough. I put the glass down on the table and lay back on the soft bed. Dad looked at me a moment, then said, "Look, Lisa, why don't we order something up here for dinner for us so you can have a quick bite then hit the sack? All this must have tired you out."

Gratefully, I agreed. Jim was right. Everything was crowding in on me—planes, cars, people, questions and the need to answer them.

As we ate dinner, Dad told me more about what had happened to Martha. She had stayed with the plane as long as she could, trying to radio for help. When the engine fire threatened explosion, she had jumped. By then, she was disoriented and miles from me. On the ground, she spent a week looking for me in the forest, then climbed as high as she could on one of the more barren mountain ridges, where she built a signal fire. She kept building fires until at the end of another week a passing plane spotted her. We had been more than a hundred miles off-course in the plane, and she was sixty miles off in the directions she gave the planes that were searching for me.

"We never expected you to show up where you did," Dad said. "You must have covered nearly a hundred miles."

"And no one knows for sure where we went down?"

"There's been no sign of the plane wreckage, but it will probably be found someday. We've got a rough idea, now, anyhow. Martha would have come to meet you," Dad said, handing me the rolls for the second time, but she was off up in the North country when the news came that you were found. She'll be back tomorrow—early—so we can have breakfast with her. Anyhow, after she got back, that's when Rex, Walter, and I went stumbling around the countryside looking for you." I looked up from my roll, which I had slathered with yellow butter. He continued. "One thing that had me really scared was I just knew you couldn't survive for long in that wild country. I'm glad—and proud—that I was dead wrong."

I swallowed, overcome with emotion for a moment, then looked up at him and said, "The worst thing was the mosquitoes."

"And the bear?"

"And the bear."

I looked down at my plate. I had eaten a steak, a baked potato, two helpings of green salad, and three rolls with butter. I was full for the first time in weeks, and it felt good.

We talked a little longer, then Dad got up and opened the door to leave. "I'm right next door, so if you can't sleep or need anything, just call me."

I hugged him and said, "Dad, I know this has been rough on you. And Mom."

Tears welled up in his eyes again as he kissed me good night and went into his own room, pulling the door shut behind him.

It felt good to be alone, to relax, to collect my thoughts. For a while, I puttered around the room, enjoying the feel of the soft carpet under my feet, the sight of the electric lights and the almost harsh colors of the room. Outside I could hear cars coming to a stop at the traffic light and an occasional honk of warning. A television set or radio was playing somewhere.

Finally, after turning off all the lights but the one by the bed, I took off the bathrobe and slid between the clean white sheets. Reaching over, I snapped off the light and lay in the dark. A deep feeling of happiness washed over me. Tonight, I thought, if I get hungry, I can pick up the phone and order from room service. I don't have to worry about bears or idiots with red beards and guns or tomorrow's meal. If it rains, I don't have to do anything about it except listen to it. And I can eat anything I want, because I am *skinny*!

The next morning, Martha was waiting for us in the hotel dining room. After hugging me, she looked me over carefully and asked, "Are you all right?"

"I'm fine. The doctor says I'm in good shape," I replied, looking at her weathered face and the long braid thrown over her shoulder. I was glad to see her.

"You're thin."

"Yes."

"You've been away a long time. Has your Dad filled you in on what happened to the rest of us?" I nodded. She said, "I don't think anybody, including you, would have thought a few weeks ago that you could do what you did."

I was a little embarrassed and tried to make light of what she had said. "The fact was I didn't have much choice," I replied, digging into my hash browns.

Martha shook her head. "Don't believe that, Lisa. People die up here in the wilderness when they get lost. It's often because they give up. You didn't."

After we ate, Martha said she had to leave to fly a hunter into the back country. "Remember," she said. "It's going to take a while for you to get used to things again. So take it easy, Lisa!"

She waved, and turned to go. Watching her push the coffee shop door open and stop to wave for one more time, I thought that it was probably the last time I would see her.

After Martha left, we went back upstairs. I called a store in the hotel to have them send up some jeans and a shirt for me to wear on the plane. "What size?" the clerk asked over the phone.

"Ten . . . no, eight," I replied. "Maybe one of each."

When the clothes came, I tried them on. The size eight jeans fit fine, were even a little roomy, and when I looked into the mirror, a different person stared back at me—thin, more big-eyed than before, not tan at all, with short hair a shade or two darker than my Los Angeles sun-bleached blond.

Later, as we passed through the lobby of the hotel on our way to the airport, reporters and photographers met us and asked me a thousand questions, which I answered as best I could. The crowd and all the loud questions made me jumpy. Dad hurried us out, and we were soon at the airport and on the plane, where I dozed most of the way to L.A. The stewardess woke me for lunch, and I saw the same food staring at me from the plastic plate as had been on the lunch menu on the Juneau flight a few weeks before. I ate it all, including the brownie.

As the plane started its descent into Los Angeles International Airport, I felt my heart give a quick jump. In a few minutes, I'd see Mother, B.J., Dave, Kyle. . . . It wasn't long before we were walking in the crowd of passengers through the covered ramp that led from plane to waiting room. I wasn't ready for the mob that was waiting. There was Mother with her eager smile and curly brown hair, B.J. jumping up and down, Dave looking serious and direct, Kyle wearing a half smile as if unsure of what expression to put on his face. . . . All those poeple, yes, but half the school as well, and again the cameras snapping and flashing and reporters yelling questions. It seemed as though everyone was hugging or laughing or crying—I joined in all three. As we started to push through the crowd, one of the reporters, louder than the rest, asked, "Will you ever go backpacking again, Miss Gallagher?"

Kyle drew himself up and answered for me. "I can tell you I'm not ever letting my girl out into any stupid forest again." He put an arm around me and looked directly into the camera.

Angry, I shrugged out from under his arm and gave my own answer to the question. "Yes, I *will* go backpacking again. Now more than ever." From the corner of my eye, I saw Kyle flush, but Dave was smiling.

Together we all walked down the long ramps into the main waiting room and over to the baggage counter, where we waited only a short while for my familiar blue pack to come riding around on the conveyor belt. I put it on my back—its weight seemed to balance me. Then we crossed the airport street to the parking lot.

Kyle spoke up as we approached the cars. "Lisa, you can ride with me. That will give us a chance to be alone." Only a few weeks before, I would have been overjoyed to hear him say that, but now I answered, "Thanks, Kyle, but I'll ride with Mom." Kyle's face turned sullen and he gave me his cold stare. When I didn't drop my eyes or speak, he stalked off to his car. He gunned the motor and drove fast out of the lot, skidding around the corner leading to the exit with a screech of tires and a spray of gravel.

B.J. said, "Well, it looks like you're over that phase."

"I'm over a lot of phases," I answered. Then I turned to the group of friends that had walked out with us. "How about everybody coming over tomorrow night, and I'll tell you about my vacation. Sorry I don't have slides." They laughed and agreed to come, as they moved off to their cars. When Dave turned to leave, too, I reached over and lay my hand on his arm. He faced me as I said, "I really used your book, Dave. It probably kept me from getting poisoned by some weird plant. And all the time I kept thinking about things you said."

"I'm glad," he answered, smiling. "We were all worried about you."

"Will you come tomorrow night?"

"I wouldn't miss it," he answered. Then he asked, "How was it really?"

"It was good *and* bad," I said, and I could tell by the look on his face that he understood.

As Mother, Dad, B.J., and I drove out onto Century Boulevard, B.J. said, "I don't know how I feel about all this. I started out the summer with an un-famous, good friend, and now I'm hobnobbing with an underfed celebrity!" The conversation was a fast mix of stories and questions and laughter until we pulled out onto the Coast Highway. The sun was low over the ocean, deep blue in the long slanting rays, and a few lavender clouds hung over the horizon. I was happy to be home.

It wasn't long before we pulled up in the driveway and into the carport. On the way into the apartment I brushed against a small tree that stood by the building, on the edge of a flowerbed that the gardener kept free of weeds. The odor of the tree made me stop. It was a small cedar I hadn't really noticed before. I reached out and pulled off a sprig and rubbed it between my fingers, then held them up to my nose to smell them. It brought it all back: the night coming in, the fire, the quiet, the tall trees seeming to guard me.

"Are you all right, Lisa?" Mom asked anxiously.

Looking up into her round, concerned face, I said, "I'm fine. Really I am." She smiled with relief and put her arm around my shoulders.

"You know, B.J.," I said. "There's one thing I want to do for sure tomorrow."

"What's that? Go to Zacky's maybe?"

"No, I'd like to go and say hello to Mrs. Zimmerman."

"Mrs. Zimmerman!"

"Right. I thought of her a lot when I was in the woods," I replied, as we climbed the stairs to our apartment door. "Do you remember, 'Let us then be up and doing, with a heart for any fate'?"

She laughed. "Sure . . . something, something, 'Life is real! Life is earnest!' That one? Longfellow?"

"It got me through a hard day, believe it or not," I said, putting down the pack by the hall closet.

Later that evening, I lay in bed, not able to sleep. The refrigerator was bumping. Mom hadn't gotten it fixed yet, I thought fondly. I heard shouting from a party down the street, a hum from the freeway, a distant stereo.

I got up, put on a bathrobe, and went outside. Streetlights cast pools of light on the dark street. It all seemed unfamiliar. Then I looked up at the stars. They were the same, though the sky had been deeper and darker in the woods, the stars brighter, seen through the tree tops. Here the stars seemed dimmed a little by the lights of Los Angeles. I stared up at them a long time, then I went back inside.

NOW YOU CAN ORDER TEMPO BOOKS BY MAIL!

Choose from this list of fine novels, every one sure to appeal to modern readers.

16494-2 A Quiet Place, by Peter Burchard $1.25
Cindy and her divorced father vacation in Maine where she meets two very different types of boys—and a quiet vacation turns into a complicated situation.

12952-3 Runaway, by Gloria D. Miklowitz $1.50
Vickie was sick of her step-father's abuse—the rules, the beatings. There was only one escape—to leave home, and soon. A dramatic and poignant story.

12951-5 Unwed Mother, by Gloria D. Miklowitz $1.50
Kathy is a teenage mother, branded and different, and she has to learn to cope with unwed motherhood while experiencing the pains of adolescence.

16492-7 Up a Road Slowly, by Irene Hunt $1.50
Winner of the Newbery Award. An honest, intimate portrayal of a 17-year-old girl's coming of age.

05421-3 Watch For a Tall White Sail, by Margaret E. Bell 95¢
Life on a remote Alaskan island is the setting for romance between a young girl and a daring young sea captain in this compelling story.

05569-4 What a Day for a Miracle, by Henry Myers 95¢
This deeply moving novel of the Children's Crusade of the 13th century is a tale of faith and cynicism, trust and betrayal, youth and age, that is extraordinarily modern in its concerns.

14594-4 When No One is Looking, by Madeline Tabler $1.50
Sixteen-year-old Sara was fleeing a broken home; Kevin was a college student on a lark. Together they travel west across the country to a commune where Sara finds herself popping pills, drinking, and doing all the things she left home to escape.

✦ **TEMPO BOOKS** Book Mailing Service
P.O. Box 690, Rockville Centre, N.Y. 11571

Please send me the titles checked above.

I enclose $_____. Add 50¢ handling fee per book.

Name_____

Address_____

City_____ State_____ Zip_____

T11A